The Girl with the Parrot on her Head

Daisy Hirst

WALKER BOOKS
AND SUBSIDIARIES
LONDON • BOSTON • SYDNEY • AUCKLAND

For Ossie

First published 2015 by Walker Books Ltd, 87 Vauxhall Walk, London SE11 5HJ
1 2 3 4 5 6 7 8 9 10 • © 2015 Daisy Hirst • The right of Daisy Hirst to be identified as author and illustrator of this work has been asserted by her in accordance with the Copyright, Designs and Patents Act 1988 • This book has been typeset in Stempel Schneidler • Printed in China • All rights reserved. No part of this book may be reproduced, transmitted or stored in an information retrieval system in any form or by any means, graphic, electronic or mechanical, including photocopying, taping and recording, without prior written permission from the publisher. • British Library Cataloguing in Publication Data: a catalogue record for this book is available from the British Library • ISBN 978-1-4063-5263-4

www.walker.co.uk

Once there was a girl with
a parrot on her head.

Her name was Isabel,
and she had a friend
called Simon

who was very good with newts.

But one day Simon
went away in a truck

and he never
came back.

For a while Isabel
hated everything.

The parrot
went to sit
on top of the
wardrobe.

Until Isabel felt quiet inside, and
decided to like being on her own.

The girl with the parrot on her head did not need friends.

She had the parrot on her head, and …

she had a system.

She sorted things out with the help
of the parrot, and pushed all the boxes
to the corner of her room.

Sometimes, at night, the parrot felt worried about the boxes, especially the box of wolves.

"Pah!" said the girl with the parrot on her head. "Don't be such a scaredy-parrot."

But secretly she was worried too –
she thought that one of the wolves
might be too big for the system.

So when she
found the biggest box
she'd ever seen, the girl with
the parrot on her head called out,
"Aha! This box is perfect for the wolf."

However,
something
was already inside.

"Oh," said Isabel.
"Is this your box?"

"Sort of," said the boy. "I was going to use it for a den."

"Why not a castle?" asked Isabel. "Why not an ostrich farm? Or a space station next to the moon?"

"No reason," said the boy, whose name was Chester. "But what did you need it for?"

Isabel explained about the wolf.

"You can't keep a wolf in a cardboard box!" said Chester. "They're supposed to live in forests far away."

"Oh," said Isabel. "Well, could you please help me tell the wolf to go?"

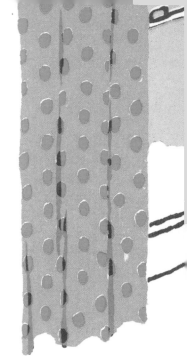

Isabel and Chester told the wolf about the forests, great plains and mountains far away, where a wolf could run and stop to howl and run again all day and night.

The wolf left at once.

"So," said Chester.
"How about this box?"

The girl with the
parrot on her head
liked being on her
own, but Chester
had a way with
umbrellas and
sticky tape

and Isabel knew
where to find martians
and helmets and string ...

and the space station
really needed *two*
astronauts

and a parrot with a teacup on its head.

FOREWORD

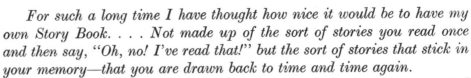

For such a long time I have thought how nice it would be to have my own Story Book. . . . Not made up of the sort of stories you read once and then say, "Oh, no! I've read that!" but the sort of stories that stick in your memory—that you are drawn back to time and time again.

Of all the stories I might have chosen, you may wonder what prompted me to choose these particular ones; and when I look for an answer I notice something. I notice that the stories, except perhaps The Snow-Child, *all end happily. We all like a story rounded off—the lost or ill-treated boy or girl finding comfort and security, ugliness turned into beauty, the eternal fairy tale where everything is possible. . . . David eventually finds his Aunt, Tom is washed and soothed, swimming about "as merry as a grig" in the cool river, the dog, Perronet, is saved by the children. There may be disappointments and much hard work, but everything turns out satisfactorily in the long run—even* The Snow-Child *tells us we must use our imagination a little and all will be well.*

So, as with all my books, making this one has been a chance for me to go back in thought to my own childhood. I have lived it over again in many of these stories and what a joy it has been to put on paper the colourful pictures which have filled my mind's eye for so long! Now when I look at them on the printed page they seem such old friends! May they be so to you!

Hilda Boswell

HILDA BOSWELL'S
TREASURY
OF
CHILDREN'S STORIES

A New Anthology of Stories for the Young
Personally selected and illustrated by Hilda Boswell

GLASGOW   COLLINS   LONDON

CONTENTS

Some of the lovely stories in this book are from classics of To-day and Yesterday; and that no one may be left wondering about the books from which they have been taken, here is a list of sources:

The story of Fairyfoot first appeared in a collection of stories called *Granny's Wonderful Chair*.

Lucy's Adventure in Narnia is part of a book called *The Lion, the Witch and the Wardrobe*.

The Road to Dover is a little bit of the life story of *David Copperfield* and tells of David's boyhood.

The Substitute is from a book called *Stuart Little,* a modern fairy tale about a jaunty little mouse-boy by an American writer.

Through the Fire is taken from a collection of stories called *On a Pincushion* which first appeared in 1876.

A day on the Alm is taken from *Heidi*, the evergreen classic of Switzerland.

Tom, the little chimney-sweep, and the story of what becomes of him is taken from the Victorian classic *The Water Babies*.

There are many other stories and poems to enchant you—not one of which will pall or lose its magic though it be read and read and read again.

Extract from *The Lion, the Witch and the Wardrobe* reprinted by permission of *Geoffrey Bles Ltd.* and *The Macmillan Company, New York*; "The Substitute" from *Stuart Little* by E. B. White. Copyright 1945 by E. B. White. Reprinted by permission of *Harper & Row, Publishers, New York*; *The Watchmaker's Shop* reprinted by permission of *Punch*.

"CHAIR OF MY GRANDMOTHER, TELL ME A STORY."

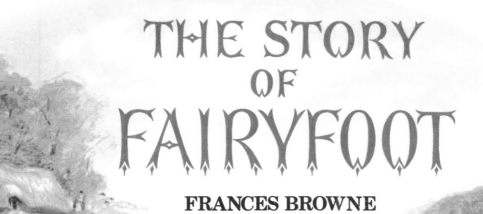

THE STORY OF FAIRYFOOT

FRANCES BROWNE

*I*n an old time, long ago, when fairies were in the world, there lived a little girl so uncommonly fair and pleasant of look, that they called her Snowflower.

Snowflower had no relation in the world but a very old grandmother, called Dame Frostyface, and they lived together in a little cottage built of peat and thatched with reeds, on the edge of a great forest. Tall trees sheltered its back from the north wind, the midday sun made its front warm and cheerful, swallows built in the eaves and daisies grew thick at the door; but there were none in all that country poorer than Snowflower and her grandmother. The only good piece of furniture in the cottage was a great armchair with wheels on its feet, a black velvet cushion, and many curious carvings of flowers and fawns on its dark oaken back.

One sunny morning, at the time of the swallows coming, the dame rose up, put on her grey hood and mantle, and said: "My child, I am going a long journey and I cannot take you with me; but the hens will lay for you, there is barley-meal in the barrel, and as you have been a good girl I'll tell you what to do when you feel lonely. Lay your head gently down on the cushion of the armchair, and say: 'Chair of my grandmother, tell me a story.' The chair was made by a cunning fairy who lived in the forest when I was young."

Having said this, Dame Frostyface set forth. Snowflower looked after the hens and cat as usual. She baked herself a cake or two of the barley-meal; but when the evening fell the cottage looked lonely. Then Snowflower remembered her grandmother's words, and laying her head gently down on the cushion she said:

"Chair of my grandmother, tell me a story."

Scarce were the words spoken, when a clear voice from under the velvet cushion began to tell a most wonderful tale.

ONCE upon a time, there stood far away in the west country, a town called Stumpinghame. It contained seven windmills, a royal palace, a market-place and a prison, with every other convenience befitting the capital of a kingdom. It was bounded on all sides by a forest so thick and old that no man in Stumpinghame knew its extent; and the opinion of the learned was that it reached to the end of the world.

There were strong reasons for this opinion. First, that forest was known to be inhabited, time out of mind, by the fairies, and no hunter cared to go beyond its borders. Secondly, the people of Stumpinghame were no travellers —man, woman and child had feet so large and heavy that it was by no means convenient to carry them far. Whether it was the nature of the place or the people I cannot tell, but great feet had been the fashion there from time immemorial, and the higher the family the larger they were. It was therefore the aim of everybody above the degree of shepherds, and such-like rustics, to swell out and enlarge their feet by way of gentility; and so successful were they in these undertakings that, at a pinch, respectable people's slippers would have served for panniers.

Stumpinghame had a king of its own and his name was Stiffstep; his family was very ancient and large-footed. His Queen, Hammer-heel, was the greatest beauty in Stumpinghame. Her majesty's shoe was not much less than a fishing-boat; their six children promised to be quite as handsome, and all went well with them till the birth of their seventh son.

For a long time nobody about the palace could understand what was the matter—the ladies-in-waiting looked so astonished, and the King so vexed; but at last it was whispered that the Queen's seventh child had been born with such miserably small feet that they resembled nothing ever heard of in Stumpinghame except the feet of the fairies.

All the relations of the King and Queen assembled at the palace to mourn with them over their singular misfortune; and to cheer up the Queen's spirits, the young Prince was sent privately out to the pasture-lands, to be nursed among the shepherds. People came from all quarters to see the young prince, and great were the lamentations over his misfortune in having such small feet.

The King and Queen had given him fourteen names, beginning with Augustus; but the honest country people could not remember so many so they called him Fairyfoot. At court, it was not thought polite to speak of him at all. They did not keep his birthday, and he was never sent for at Christmas because the Queen and her ladies could not bear the sight. Once a year the undermost scullion was sent to see how he did, with a bundle of his next brother's cast-off clothes; and as the King grew old and cross it was said he had thoughts of disowning him.

So Fairyfoot grew in Shepherd Fleecefold's cottage. Perhaps the country air made him fair and rosy—for all agreed that he would have been a handsome boy but for his small feet, with which, nevertheless, he learned to walk, and in time to run and jump, thereby amazing everybody, for such doings were not known among the children of Stumpinghame. Fairyfoot was, however, despised among the shepherds. The old people thought him unlucky; the children refused to play with him. Every day, he was sent to watch some sickly sheep that grazed on a wild, weedy pasture, hard by the forest.

Poor Fairyfoot was often lonely and sorrowful; and many a time he wished his feet would grow larger. He was lying in the shadow of a mossy rock one warm summer's noon, with the sheep feeding around, when a robin, pursued by a great hawk, flew into the old velvet cap which lay on the ground beside him. Fairyfoot covered it up, and the hawk, frightened by his shout, flew away.

"Now you may go, poor robin!" he said, opening the cap; but instead of the bird, out sprang a little man dressed in russet brown, and looking as if he were a hundred years old.

"Thank you for your shelter, and be sure I will do as much for you. Call on me if you are ever in trouble; my name is Robin Goodfellow." And darting off, he was out of sight in an instant.

Fairyfoot kept the story to himself, for the little man's feet were as small as his own, and it was clear he would be no favourite in Stumpinghame.

At last midsummer came. That evening was a feast among the shepherds. But Fairyfoot sat alone beside his sheepfold, for the children of his village had refused to let him dance with them about the bonfire. Fairyfoot had never felt so lonely in all his life, and remembering the little man, he plucked up spirit and cried;

"Ho, Robin Goodfellow!"

"Here I am!" said a shrill voice; and there stood the little man himself.

"I am very lonely, and no one will play with me because my feet are not large enough," said Fairyfoot.

"Come then and play with us," said the little man. "We care for nobody's feet. But there is one thing you must mind among us: never speak of anything you may hear or see, for we and the people of this country have had no friend-ship ever since large feet came into fashion."

The little man led Fairyfoot into the forest, and along a mossy path among old trees wreathed with ivy, till they heard the sound of music and came upon a meadow where the moon shone as bright as day, and all the flowers of the year bloomed together in the thick grass. There was a crowd of little men and women, some clad in russet colour, but far more in green, dancing round a little well as clear as crystal. And under great rose trees which grew here and there in the meadow, companies were sitting round low tables covered with cups of milk, dishes of honey and carved wooden flagons filled with clear red wine. The little man led Fairyfoot up to the nearest table, handed him one of the flagons and said:

"Drink to the good company!"

The boy had never tasted such a drink as that before; for scarcely had it gone down, when he forgot all his troubles. Fairyfoot was as happy as a prince and danced with the little people till the moon was low in the sky. Then the little man took him by the hand, and never stopped nor stayed till he was at his own bed of straw in the cottage corner.

Every night all that summer the little man came and took him away to dance in the forest. The wonder was that he was never tired nor sleepy; but before the summer was ended, Fairyfoot found out the reason. One night when the moon was full and the last of the ripe corn rustling in the fields, Robin Goodfellow came for him as usual, and away they went to the flowery green. The fun was high and they were in haste to join the dance, so Fairyfoot did not drink the clear red wine from the carved cup. Never in all his life did Fairyfoot find such hard work as to keep pace with the company. At length he was glad to steal away and sit down behind a mossy oak, where his eyes closed for very weariness.

When he awoke, two little ladies clad in green talked beside him.

"What a beautiful boy!" said one of them. "He is worthy to be a king's son. Only see what handsome feet he has!"

"Yes," said the other, with a laugh that sounded spiteful; "they are just like the feet Princess Maybloom had before she washed them in the Growing Well. Her father has sent far and wide throughout the whole country searching for a doctor to make them small again, but nothing in this world can do it except the water of the Fair Fountain, and none but I and the nightingales know where it is."

"One would not care to let the like be known," said the first little lady; "there would come such crowds of these great coarse creatures of mankind, nobody would have peace for leagues round. But you will surely send word to the sweet princess!"

"Not I, indeed!" said the spiteful fairy. "Her old skinflint of a father cut down the cedar which I loved best in the whole forest, and made a chest of it to hold his money in."

When Robin Goodfellow came to take him home, Fairyfoot did not let him know that he had overheard anything. All next day he was so weary that in the afternoon he fell asleep. Towards evening, the old shepherd thought he would see how things went on in the pastures, and no sooner did he catch sight of Fairyfoot sleeping and his flock straying away, than shouting all the ill names he could remember, in a voice which woke the boy, he ran after him as fast as his great feet would allow; while Fairyfoot fled into the forest and never stopped till he reached the banks of a little stream.

He followed the stream for many an hour as it wound away into the heart of the forest, leading Fairyfoot at last, when he was tired and the night had fallen, to a grove of great rose trees with thousands of nightingales singing in the branches. In the midst of the grove was a clear spring bordered with lilies and Fairyfoot sat down by it to rest. As he sat, the nightingales began to talk together.

"What boy is that?" said one. "He cannot have come from Stumpinghame with such small and handsome feet."

"No," said another, "he has come from the west country. How in the world did he find the way?"

"How simple you are!" said a third nightingale. "What had he to do but follow the ground-ivy which grows over height and hollow, bank and bush, from the lowest gate of the King's kitchen garden to the root of this rose tree?"

When the talking ceased, Fairyfoot thought it might be as well for him to follow the ground-ivy, and see the Princess Maybloom. It was a long journey, but he went on, never losing sight of the ground-ivy which led him over height and hollow, bank and bush, out of the forest and along a noble high road to a great city, and a low, old-fashioned gate of the King's kitchen garden which had not been opened for seven years.

The gate was overgrown with tall weeds and moss, so the boy climbed over. A dappled fawn came frisking by, and he heard a soft, sorrowful voice saying:

"Come back, come back, my fawn! I cannot run and play with you now, my feet have grown so heavy."

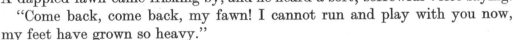

Looking round, he saw the loveliest Princess in the world, dressed in snow white, and wearing a wreath of roses on her golden hair; but walking slowly, as the great people did in Stumpinghame, for her feet were as large as the best of them. At once he guessed that this must be the Princess Maybloom.

"Royal Princess," said Fairyfoot, making a humble bow, "I have heard of your trouble because your feet have grown large; but I know of a certain fountain that will make them smaller and finer than ever they were, if the King, your father, gives you leave to come with me, accompanied by two of your maids that are the least given to talking, and the most prudent officer in the royal household; for it would grievously offend the fairies and the nightingales to make the fountain known."

When the Princess heard that, she danced for joy in spite of her large feet, and she brought Fairyfoot before the King and Queen. At first the King would not believe that there could be any use in his offer, because so many great physicians had failed to give any relief; but the Queen, being a prudent woman, said:

"I pray your majesty to notice what fine feet this boy has. There may be some truth in his story."

After some persuasion the King consented. So the two silent maids, the discreet chamberlain and the fawn, which would not stay behind, were sent with Princess Maybloom. Fairyfoot had hard work guiding them along the track of the ground-ivy. The maids and the chamberlain did not like the brambles and the rough roots of the forest; but the Princess went on with good courage, and at last they reached the grove of rose trees, and the spring bordered with lilies.

The moment the Princess's feet touched the water they grew less, and when she had washed and dried them three times, they were as small and finely shaped as Fairyfoot's own.

"Oh," said Fairyfoot sorrowfully, "if there had been a well in the world to make my feet large, my father and mother would not have cast me off, nor sent me to live among the shepherds."

"Cheer up your heart," said the Princess Maybloom. "If you want large feet there is a well in this forest that will do it. Last summer I washed my feet in the well; but as I washed they grew larger every minute, and nothing could ever make them less again. As you have shown me the Fair Fountain, I will show you the Growing Well."

Up rose Fairyfoot and Princess Maybloom, and went together till they found the muddy-looking well in the deepest dell of the forest. Fairyfoot sat down to wash, but at that minute he heard a sound of music, and knew it was the fairies going to their dancing ground.

"If my feet grow large," said the boy to himself, "how shall I dance with them?" So rising quickly, he took the Princess Maybloom by the hand. The fawn followed them; the maids and the chamberlain followed it, and all followed the music through the forest, till they came to the flowery green. Robin Goodfellow welcomed the company for Fairyfoot's sake and gave everyone a drink of the fairies' wine. So they danced there from sunset till the grey morning; but before the lark sang, Robin Goodfellow took them all safe home.

There was great joy that day in the palace because Princess Maybloom's feet were made small again. The King gave Fairyfoot all manner of fine clothes and rich jewels; and in process of time, Fairyfoot and Princess Maybloom were married, and still live happily. When they go to visit at Stumpinghame, they always wash their feet in the Growing Well, lest the royal family might think them a disgrace, but when they come back, they make haste to the Fair Fountain; and the fairies and the nightingales are great friends to them, as well as the maids and the chamberlain, because they have told nobody about it, and there is peace and quiet yet in the grove of rose trees.

LUCY'S ADVENTURE IN NARNIA

C. S. LEWIS

ONCE there were four children whose names were Peter, Susan, Edmund and Lucy. They were sent away from London during the war to the house of an old professor who lived in the heart of the country. It was the sort of house that you never seem to come to the end of, and it was full of unexpected places. One room was quite empty except for a big wardrobe.

"Nothing there!" said Peter as they explored the house. Lucy stayed behind because she thought it would be worth while trying the door of the wardrobe. To her surprise, it opened quite easily. She stepped inside among several long fur coats which were hanging there, for there was nothing she liked so much as the smell and feel of fur. Of course, she left the door open because she knew it was very foolish to shut oneself into any wardrobe. It was almost quite dark and she kept her arms stretched out in front of her so as not to bump her face into the back of the wardrobe.

"This must be a simply enormous wardrobe!" thought Lucy, going still further in. Then she noticed that there was something crunching under her feet. "I wonder is it moth-balls?" she thought, stooping down to feel it with her hands. But instead of feeling hard, smooth wood, she felt something soft and powdery and extremely cold. "This is very queer," she said.

Next moment she found that what was rubbing against her face and hands was no longer soft fur but something hard and rough and even prickly. "Why, it is just like branches of trees!" exclaimed Lucy. And then she saw that there was a light ahead of her; not a few inches away where the back of the wardrobe ought to have been, but a long way off. A moment later she found that she was standing in the middle of a wood at night-time with snow under her feet and snowflakes falling through the air.

Lucy felt a little frightened, but she felt very inquisitive and excited as well. She looked back over her shoulder and there, between the dark tree-trunks, she could still see the open doorway of the wardrobe. "I can always get back if anything goes wrong," thought Lucy.

In about ten minutes she reached the light and found it was a lamp-post. As she stood looking at it, wondering why there was a lamp-post in the middle of a wood, she heard a pitter patter of feet coming towards her. And soon after that a very strange person stepped out from among the trees. He was only a little taller than Lucy herself and he carried over his head an umbrella, white with snow. From the waist upwards he was like a man, but his legs were shaped like a goat's (the hair on them was glossy and black) and instead of feet he had goat's hoofs. He also had a tail, but Lucy did not notice this at first because it was neatly caught up over the arm that held the umbrella so as to keep it from trailing in the snow. He had a red woollen muffler round his neck and his skin was rather reddish too. He had a strange but pleasant little face, with a short pointed beard and curly hair, and out of the hair there stuck two horns, one on each side of his forehead. When he saw Lucy he gave a start of surprise.

"Goodness gracious me!" exclaimed the faun.

"Good evening," said Lucy. The faun made her a little bow.

"Good evening, good evening. Should I be right in thinking that you are a Daughter of Eve?"

"My name's Lucy," said she, not quite understanding him.

"But you are what they call a girl?" asked the faun.

"Of course I'm a girl," said Lucy.

"You are, in fact, human?"

"Of course I'm human," said Lucy.

"To be sure, to be sure," said the faun. "How stupid of me! But I've never seen a Son of Adam or a Daughter of Eve before. I am delighted. Allow me to introduce myself. My name is Tumnus. May I ask, O, Lucy Daughter of Eve, how you have come into Narnia?"

"Narnia?" said Lucy.

"This is the land of Narnia," said the faun. "Have you come from the wild woods of the west?"

"I—I got in through the wardrobe in the spare room," said Lucy.

"Ah!" said Mr. Tumnus, "if only I had worked harder at geography when I was a little faun, I should no doubt know all about those strange countries."

"But they aren't countries at all," said Lucy. "It's only just back there—at least—I'm not sure. It is summer there."

"Meanwhile," said Mr. Tumnus, "it is winter in Narnia, and has been for ever so long, and we shall both catch cold if we stand here talking in the snow. Daughter of Eve from the far land of Spare Oom where eternal summer reigns around the bright city of War Drobe, how would it be if you came and had tea with me?"

"Thank you very much, Mr. Tumnus," said Lucy. "But I was wondering whether I ought to be getting back."

"It's only just round the corner," said the faun, "and there'll be a roaring fire—and toast—and sardines—and cake."

"Well, it's very kind of you," said Lucy.

"If you will take my arm, Daughter of Eve," said Mr. Tumnus, "I shall be able to hold the umbrella over both of us."

And so Lucy found herself walking through the wood arm in arm with this strange creature as if they had known one another all their lives.

They had not gone far before they came to a place where the ground became rough. Mr. Tumnus turned suddenly aside as if he were going to walk straight into an unusually large rock, but at the last moment Lucy found he was leading her into the entrance of a cave. As soon as they were inside she found herself blinking in the light of a wood fire. Then Mr. Tumnus stooped and took a flaming piece of wood out of the fire with a neat little pair of tongs, and lit a lamp. "Now we shan't be long," he said, and immediately put a kettle on.

Lucy thought she had never been in a nicer place. It was a little dry, clean cave of reddish stone with a carpet on the floor and two little chairs and a table and a dresser and a mantelpiece over the fire and above that a picture of an old faun with a grey beard.

Mr. Tumnus set out the tea things. "Now, Daughter of Eve!" he said. And really it was a wonderful tea. There was a nice brown egg, lightly boiled, for each of them, and then sardines on toast, and then buttered toast, and then toast with honey, and then a sugar-topped cake. And when Lucy was tired of eating the faun began to talk. He had wonderful tales to tell of life in the forest. Then he took from its case on the dresser a strange little flute that looked as if it were made of straw, and began to play. And the tune he played made Lucy want to cry and laugh and dance and go to sleep all at the same time. It must have been hours later when she shook herself and said:

"Oh, Mr. Tumnus, I really must go home. I only meant to stay for a few minutes."

"It's no good *now*, you know," said the faun, laying down its flute and shaking its head at her very sorrowfully.

"No good?" said Lucy, jumping up. "What do you mean? I've got to go home at once. The others will be wondering what has happened to me." But a moment later she asked, "Mr. Tumnus! Whatever is the matter?" for the faun's brown eyes had filled with tears and then the tears began to trickle down its cheeks, and at last it covered its face with its hands and began to howl.

"Mr. Tumnus!" said Lucy in great distress. "Do tell me what is wrong." But the faun continued sobbing as if its heart would break. "Mr. Tumnus!" bawled Lucy in his ear. "Stop it at once! What on earth are you crying about?"

"Oh—oh—oh!" sobbed Mr. Tumnus, "I'm crying because I'm such a bad faun."

"I don't think you're a bad faun at all," said Lucy. "You are the nicest faun I've ever met."

"Oh—oh—you wouldn't say that if you knew," replied Mr. Tumnus between his sobs.

"But what have you done?" asked Lucy.

"Taken service under the White Witch. I'm in the pay of the White Witch. It is she that has got all Narnia under her thumb. It's she that makes it always winter. Always winter and never Christmas; think of that!"

"How awful!" said Lucy. "But what does she pay *you* for?"

"I'm a kidnapper for her, that's what I am," said Mr. Tumnus with a deep groan. "Look at me, Daughter of Eve. Would you believe that I'm the sort of faun to meet a poor innocent child in the wood, pretend to be friendly with it, and invite it home to my cave, all for the sake of lulling it asleep and then handing it over to the White Witch?"

"No," said Lucy. "I'm sure you wouldn't do anything of the sort."

"But I have," said the faun.

"Well," said Lucy slowly, "well, that was pretty bad. But you're so sorry for it that I'm sure you will never do it again."

"Daughter of Eve, don't you understand?" said the faun. "I'm doing it now."

"What do you mean?" cried Lucy, turning very white.

"You are the child," said Tumnus. "I had orders from the White Witch that if ever I saw a Son of Adam or a Daughter of Eve in the wood, I was to catch them and hand them over to her. And you are the first I ever met."

"Oh, but you won't, Mr. Tumnus," said Lucy. "You won't, will you?"

"If I don't," said he, beginning to cry again, "she's sure to find out. She'll turn me into stone and I shall be only a statue of a faun."

"I'm very sorry, Mr. Tumnus," said Lucy. "But please let me go home."

"Of course I will," said the faun. "I hadn't known what humans were like before I met you. We must go as quietly as we can. The whole wood is full of *her* spies."

The journey back was not at all like the journey to the faun's cave; they stole along as quickly as they could, without speaking a word, and Mr. Tumnus kept to the darkest places. Lucy was relieved when they reached the lamp-post again.

She looked very hard between the trees and could just see in the distance a patch of light that looked like daylight. "I can see the wardrobe door," she said.

"Farewell, Daughter of Eve," said the faun. "C-can you ever forgive me?"

"Why, of course I can," said Lucy. "And I do hope you won't get into dreadful trouble on my account," and she ran towards the far-off patch of daylight as quickly as her legs would carry her.

Presently, instead of rough branches brushing past her she felt coats, and instead of crunching snow under her feet she felt wooden boards, and all at once she found herself jumping out of the wardrobe into the same empty room from which the adventure had started. She shut the wardrobe door tightly behind her. She could hear the voices of the others in the passage.

"I'm here," she shouted. "I've come back. I'm all right!"

TWO PEOPLE OF FIFE

In a cottage near Fife,
Lived a man and his wife,
Who, believe me, were comical folk;
For to people's surprise,
They both saw with their eyes,
And their tongues moved, whenever they spoke.

What's amazing to tell,
I have heard that their smell
Chiefly lay in a thing called their nose.
And, though strange are such tales,
On their fingers they'd nails,
As well as on each of their toes.

When quite fast asleep,
I've been told that to keep
Their eyes open they scarce could contrive;
They walked on their feet,
And 'twas thought, what they eat
Helped, with drinking, to keep them alive.

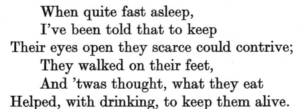

THE ROAD TO DOVER

CHARLES DICKENS

Little David Copperfield, an orphan, and ill-treated by his step-father, is sent to work in a bottling factory in London, where his only friends are the Micawber family. He is ten years old.

MR. and Mrs. Micawber and their family were going away from London, and a parting between us was near at hand. I had grown so accustomed to the Micawbers, and was so utterly friendless without them, that I felt my life was unendurable. It was in my walk home one night and the sleepless hours which followed when I lay in bed, that the thought first occurred to me to run away. To go, by some means or other, down into the country, to the only relation I had in the world, and tell my story to my aunt, Miss Betsey Trotwood.

As I did not even know where Miss Betsey lived, I wrote a letter to my old nurse, Peggotty, asking her if she remembered, and saying I had a particular occasion for half-a-guinea; and that if she could lend me that sum until I could repay it, I should be very much obliged to her, and would tell her afterwards what I had wanted it for.

Peggotty's answer soon arrived, and was, as usual, full of affection. She enclosed the half-guinea and told me that Miss Betsey lived near Dover.

I resolved to set out at the end of that week.

My box was still at my old lodging and I looked about me for some one who would help me to carry it to the booking-office. There was a long-legged young man with a very little empty donkey-cart, standing in the Blackfriars Road, whose eye I caught as I was going by. I asked whether he might or might not like a job.

"Wot job?" said the long-legged young man.

"To move a box," I answered.

"Wot box?" said the long-legged young man.

I told him mine, which was down that street there, and which I wanted him to take to the Dover coach-office for sixpence.

"Done with you for a tanner!" said the long-legged young man, and directly got upon his cart and rattled away at such a rate, that it was as much as I could do to keep pace with the donkey.

There was a defiant manner about this young man that I did not much like; as the bargain was made, however, I took him upstairs to the room I was leaving, and we brought the box down and put it on his cart; and he rattled away as if he, my box, the cart, and the donkey, were all equally mad; and I was quite out of breath with calling and running after him, when I caught him at the coach-office.

Being much flushed and excited, I tumbled my half-guinea out of my pocket; so I put it in my mouth for safety, and had just tied the direction-card on my box when I felt myself violently chucked under the chin by the long-legged young man, and saw my half-guinea fly out of my mouth into his hand.

"You give me my money back, if you please," said I, very much frightened; but he jumped into the cart, sat upon my box, and rattled away harder than ever.

I ran after him as fast as I could. "Give me my box and money, will you?" I cried, bursting into tears.

I narrowly escaped being run over, twenty times at least, in half a mile. At length, confused by fright and heat, I left the young man to go where he would with my box and money; and, panting and crying, but never stopping, faced about for Greenwich, which I had understood was on the Dover road.

For anything I know, I may have had some wild idea of running all the way to Dover, but I came to a stop in the Kent Road where I sat down on a door-step. It was by this time dark; I heard the clocks strike ten. But it was a summer night and fine weather. When I had recovered my breath I trudged on miserably until I happened to pass a little shop, where it was written up that ladies' and gentlemen's wardrobes were bought. The master of this shop was sitting at the door in his shirt-sleeves, smoking. I went up the next by-street, took off my waist-coat, rolled it neatly under my arm, and came back to the shop-door. "If you please, sir," I said, "I am to sell this for a fair price."

He took the waist-coat, stood his pipe upon its head against the door-post, went into the shop, followed by me, spread the waist-coat on the counter, and looked at it there, held it up against the light and looked at it there.

"What do you call a price, now, for this here little weskit?" he said.

"Would eighteenpence be—?" I hinted.

"I should rob my family if I was to offer ninepence for it," he said and gave it me back.

I said I would take ninepence for it, if he pleased. Not without some grumbling, he gave ninepence. I buttoned my jacket and set off once again, with my ninepence in my pocket.

Never shall I forget the lonely sensation of first lying down without a roof above my head! I found a haystack and lay down by it and slept until the warm beams of the sun woke me. Then I crept away and struck into the long dusty track which I knew to be the Dover road. I heard the church-bells ringing, as I plodded on; and I passed a church or two where the congregation were inside, and the sound of singing came out into the sunshine. I felt quite wicked in my dirt and dust, and with my tangled hair.

I got, that Sunday, through three-and-twenty miles, and toiling into Chatham, crept, at last, upon a sort of grass-grown battery overhanging a lane. Here I lay down and slept soundly until morning.

Very stiff and sore of foot I was in the morning, and feeling that I could go but a very little way that day, I resolved to make the sale of my jacket its principal business. It was a likely place to sell a jacket in; for the dealers in second-hand clothes were numerous. At last I found one that I thought looked promising, at the corner of a dirty lane. Into this shop I went with a palpitating heart; which was not relieved when an ugly old man, with the lower part of his face all covered with a stubbly grey beard, rushed out of a dirty den behind it, and seized me by the hair of my head. He was a dreadful old man to look at, in a filthy flannel waistcoat, and smelling terribly of rum.

"Oh, what do you want?" he said. "Oh, my eyes and limbs, what do you want? Oh, my lungs and liver, what do you want? Oh, goroo, goroo!"

"I wanted to know," I said, trembling, "if you would buy a jacket."

"Oh, let's see the jacket!" cried the old man. "Oh, my heart on fire, show the jacket to us!"

With that he took his trembling hands, which were like the claws of a great bird, out of my hair.

"Oh, how much for the jacket?" cried the old man, after examining it. "Oh, goroo!—how much for the jacket?"

"Half-a-crown," I answered.

"Oh, my lungs and liver," cried the old man, "no! Oh, my eyes, no! Oh, my limbs, no! Eighteenpence. Goroo!"

"Well," said I, "I'll take eighteenpence."

"Oh, my liver!" cried the old man, throwing the jacket on a shelf. "Get out of the shop! Oh, my lungs, get out of the shop! Oh, my eyes and limbs—goroo!"

I never was so frightened in my life, before or since. So I went outside and sat down in the shade in a corner. And I sat there so many hours that the shade became sunlight, and the sunlight became shade again, and still I sat there waiting for the money. He made many attempts to induce me to consent to an exchange; at one time coming out with a fishing-rod, at another with a fiddle, at another with a cocked hat, at another with a flute. But I sat there in desperation; each time asking him, with tears in my eyes, for my money or my jacket. At last he began to pay me in halfpence at a time; and was full two hours getting by easy stages to a shilling.

"Oh, my eyes and limbs!" he then cried, "will you go for twopence more?"

"I can't," I said; "I shall be starved."

"Oh, my lungs and liver, will you go for threepence?"

"I would go for nothing, if I could," I said, "but I want the money badly."

"Oh, go—roo! Will you go for fourpence?"

I was so faint and weary that I closed with this offer; and taking the money out of his claw, went away more hungry and thirsty than I had ever been, a little before sunset. But at an expense of threepence I soon refreshed myself completely; and being in better spirits then, limped seven miles upon my road.

My bed at night was under another haystack, where I rested comfortably, after having washed my blistered feet in a stream. When I took the road again next morning, I found that it lay through hop-grounds and orchards. The orchards were ruddy with ripe apples, and in a few places the hop-pickers were already at work. I thought it all extremely beautiful, and made up my mind to sleep among the hops that night.

There were many trampers on the road next day. Some of them were most ferocious-looking ruffians, who stared at me as I went by. One young fellow, a tinker, roared to me in such a tremendous voice to come back, that I halted and looked round.

"Where are you going?" said the tinker, gripping my shirt with his blackened hand.

"I am going to Dover," I said.

"Where do you come from?" asked the tinker, giving his hand another turn in my shirt, to hold me more securely.

"I come from London," I said.

He made as though to strike me, then looked at me from head to foot.

"What do you mean," said the tinker, "by wearing my brother's silk hand-kercher? Give it over here!" And he had mine off my neck in a moment.

This adventure frightened me so, that, afterwards, when I saw any of these people coming, I turned back until I could find a hiding-place, where I remained until they had gone out of sight.

I came at last upon the bare, wide downs near Dover; and on the sixth day of my flight, there I stood with my ragged shoes, and my dusty, sunburnt, half-clothed figure, in the place so long desired.

I inquired about my aunt among the boatmen first; then the fly-drivers and the shopkeepers. I was sitting on the step of an empty shop at a street-corner, near the market-place, when a fly-driver, coming by with his carriage, dropped a horse-cloth. As I handed it up, I asked him if he could tell me where Miss Trotwood lived; though I had asked the question so often, that it almost died upon my lips.

"Old lady?" said he.

"Yes," I said, "rather."

"Pretty stiff in the back?" said he.

"Yes," I said. "I should think it very likely."

"Gruffish and comes down upon you sharp?"

My heart sank within me.

"Why then, I tell you what," said he. "If you go up there," pointing with his whip towards the heights, "and keep right on till you come to some houses facing the sea, I think you'll hear of her. My opinion is, she won't stand anything, so here's a penny for you."

I accepted the gift thankfully, and bought a loaf with it. I went in the direction my friend had indicated, and at length I saw a little shop and inquired if they could tell me where Miss Trotwood lived. A young woman, who was buying some rice, turned round quickly.

"My mistress?" she said. "What do you want with her, boy?"

"I want," I replied, "to speak to her, if you please."

My aunt's maid put her rice in a little basket and walked out of the shop; telling me that I could follow her. I followed the young woman, and we soon came to a very neat little cottage.

"This is Miss Trotwood's," said the young woman. "Now you know," and left me standing at the garden-gate.

I lifted up my eyes to the window above where I saw a pleasant-looking gentleman, who shut up one eye, nodded his head at me several times, laughed,

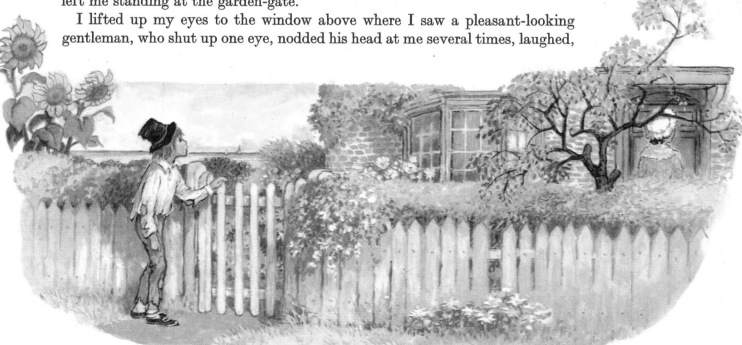

and went away. Then there came out of the house a lady with a handkerchief tied over her cap, and a pair of gardening gloves on her hands. I knew her immediately to be Miss Betsey, for she came stalking out of the house exactly as my poor mother had so often described her.

"Go away!" said Miss Betsey, shaking her head. "Go along! No boys here!"

With my heart at my lips, I went softly in and stood beside her as she stooped to dig up some little root.

"If you please, ma'am," I began.

She started and looked up.

"If you please, aunt."

"EH?" exclaimed Miss Betsey, in a tone of amazement.

"If you please, aunt, I am your nephew."

My aunt sat flat down on the garden-path. She stared at me until I began to cry; when she got up in a great hurry, collared me, and took me into the parlour. As I was quite unable to control my sobs, she put me on the sofa, exclaiming at intervals, "Mercy on us!"

After a time she rang the bell. "Janet," said my aunt when her servant came in. "Go upstairs, give my compliments to Mr. Dick, and say I wish to speak to him." The gentleman who had squinted at me from the upper window came in laughing.

"Mr. Dick," said my aunt, "don't be a fool."

The gentleman was serious immediately.

"Mr. Dick," said my aunt, "you have heard me mention David Copperfield."

"David Copperfield?" said Mr. Dick, who did not appear to me to remember much about it. "Oh, yes, to be sure. David, certainly."

"Well," said my aunt, "this is his boy—his son, and he has done a pretty piece of business. He has run away. Now, the question I put to you is, what shall I do with him?"

"What shall you do with him?" said Mr. Dick, feebly, scratching his head. "Oh! do with him?"

"Yes," said my aunt, with a grave look, and her forefinger held up. "Come! I want some very sound advice."

"Why, if I was you," said Mr. Dick, considering, "I should—I should wash him!"

"Janet," said my aunt, "Mr. Dick sets us all right. Heat the bath!"

The bath was a great comfort. For I began to feel pains in my limbs from lying out in the fields, and was now so tired that I could hardly keep myself awake for five minutes together. When I had bathed, they dressed me in a shirt and a pair of trousers belonging to Mr. Dick, and tied me up in two or three great shawls. What sort of bundle I looked like, I don't know, but I felt a very hot one. Feeling also very faint and drowsy, I soon lay down on the sofa again and fell asleep.

We dined soon after I awoke, off a roast fowl and a pudding; I sitting at table, not unlike a trussed bird myself, and moving my arms with considerable difficulty. All this time, I was deeply anxious to know what my aunt was going to do with me; but she took her dinner in silence, except when she fixed her eyes on me sitting opposite and said, "Mercy upon us!"

Afterwards, we sat at the window until dusk, when Janet set candles on the table, and pulled down the blinds.

"Now, Mr. Dick," said my aunt, with her grave look. "I am going to ask you another question. Look at this child."

"David's son?" said Mr. Dick, with a puzzled face.

"Exactly so," returned my aunt. "What would you do with him, now?"

"Do with David's son," said Mr. Dick. "Oh! Yes. Do with—I should put him to bed."

"Janet!" cried my aunt. "Mr. Dick sets us all right. If the bed is ready, we'll take him up to it."

The room was a pleasant one, at the top of the house, overlooking the sea, on which the moon was shining brilliantly. After I had said my prayers, and the candle had burnt out, I remember how I still sat looking at the moonlight on the water, as if I could hope to read my fortune in it. I remember how I turned my eyes away, and the feeling of gratitude which the sight of the white-curtained bed and the snow-white sheets inspired. I remember how I thought of all the solitary places under the night sky where I had slept, and how I prayed that I never might be houseless any more. I remember how I seemed to float down the moonlit glory of that track upon the sea, away into the world of dreams.

THE REAL PRINCESS

HANS ANDERSEN

THERE was once a Prince who wished to marry a Princess; but, he said, she must be a *real* Princess. He travelled all over the world in hopes of finding such a lady; but there was always something wrong. Princesses he found in plenty; but whether they were real Princesses it was impossible for him to decide, for now one thing, now another, seemed to him not quite right about the ladies. At last he returned to his palace quite cast down, because he wished so much to have a real Princess for his wife.

One evening a fearful tempest arose. It thundered and lightened, and the rain poured down from the sky in torrents; besides, it was as dark as pitch. All at once there was heard a violent knocking at the door, and the old King, the Prince's father, went out himself to open it.

It was a Princess who was standing outside the door. What with the rain and the wind, she was in a sad condition. The water trickled down from her hair, and her clothes clung to her body. She said she was a real Princess.

"Ah, we shall soon see that!" thought the old Queen-mother. However, she said not a word of what she was going to do; but went quietly into the bedroom, took all the bed-clothes off the bed, and put three little peas on the bedstead. She then laid twenty mattresses one upon another over the three peas, and put twenty feather beds over the mattresses.

Upon this the princess was to pass the night.

The next morning she was asked how she had slept. "Oh, very badly indeed!" she replied. "I have scarcely closed my eyes the whole night through. I do not know what was in my bed, but I had something hard under me, and am all over black and blue. It has hurt me so much!"

Now it was plain that the lady must be a real Princess, since she had been able to feel the three little peas through the twenty mattresses and twenty feather beds. None but a real Princess could have had such a delicate sense of feeling.

The Prince accordingly made her his wife; being now convinced that he had found a real Princess. The three peas were, however, put into the cabinet of curiosities, where they are still to be seen, provided they are not lost.

Was not this a lady of real delicacy?

The Substitute

E. B. WHITE

A story about the mouse-boy who became a school-teacher for a day.

THE home of the Little family was a pleasant place near a park in New York City.

When Mrs. Little's second son was born, everybody noticed that he was not much bigger than a mouse. The truth of the matter was the baby looked very much like a mouse in every way. He was only about two inches high; and he had a mouse's sharp nose, a mouse's tail, a mouse's whiskers, and the pleasant, shy manner of a mouse. Mr. and Mrs. Little named him Stuart, and Mr. Little made him a tiny bed out of four clothes-pins and a cigarette box. Unlike most babies, Stuart could walk as soon as he was born. Mrs. Little saw right away that the baby clothes she had provided were unsuitable, and she set to work and made him a fine little blue worsted suit with patch pockets in which he could keep his handkerchief, his money, and his keys.

Stuart was an early riser: he was almost always the first person up in the morning. One fine spring morning when Stuart was three years old, he decided that he would leave home without telling anybody and go out into the world.

He got into his car (a miniature one his friend the Doctor had given him) and started early to avoid the traffic. He drove through Central Park and over to the West Side Highway. The car ran beautifully, and although the people were inclined to stare at him, Stuart didn't mind. Just as the sun was coming up, he saw a man seated in thought by the side of the road. Stuart steered his car alongside, stopped, and put his head out.

"You're worried about something, aren't you?" asked Stuart.

"Yes, I am," said the man.

"Can I help you in any way?" asked Stuart in a friendly voice.

The man shook his head. "You see, I'm the Superintendent of Schools. One of my teachers is ill—Miss Gunderson her name is. She teaches Class Four. I've got to find a substitute for her, a teacher who will take her place."

"What's the matter with her?" asked Stuart.

"I don't know exactly. The doctor says she may have rhinestones," replied the Superintendent.

"Can't you find another teacher?" asked Stuart.

"No, that's the trouble. And school is supposed to begin in an hour."

"I will be glad to take Miss Gunderson's place for a day, if you would like," suggested Stuart agreeably.

The Superintendent looked up.

"Really?"

"Certainly," said Stuart. "Glad to." He opened the door of the little car and stepped out. Walking round to the rear, he took out his suitcase. "If I'm to conduct a class in a schoolroom, I'd better get into something more suitable," he said.

Stuart climbed the bank, went into the bushes, and was back in a few minutes wearing a pepper-and-salt jacket, old striped trousers, a bow tie, and spectacles. He folded his other clothes and packed them away in the suitcase.

"Do you think you can maintain discipline?" asked the Superintendent.

"Of course I can," replied Stuart. "I'll make the work interesting and the discipline will take care of itself. Don't worry about me."

At quarter to nine the scholars had gathered in Class Four. When they missed Miss Gunderson and word got round that there would be a substitute, they were delighted.

"A Substitute!" somebody whispered to somebody else. "A Substitute! A Substitute!"

Stuart arrived at nine. He parked his car briskly at the door of the school, stalked boldly into the room, found a pointer leaning against Miss Gunderson's desk, and climbed hand-over-hand to the top. There he found an ink-well, some pens and pencils, some chalk, a bell, and three or four books in a pile. Stuart scrambled nimbly up to the top of the stack of books and jumped for the button on the bell. His weight was enough to make it ring, and Stuart promptly slid down, walked to the front of the desk, and said:

"Let me have your attention, please!"

The boys and girls crowded around the desk to look at the substitute. Everyone talked at once, and they seemed to be very much pleased. The girls giggled and the boys laughed and everyone's eyes lit up with excitement to see such a small and good-looking teacher, so appropriately dressed.

"Let me have your attention, please!" repeated Stuart. "As you know, Miss Gunderson is ill and I am taking her place."

"What's the matter with her?" asked Roy Hart, eagerly.

"Vitamin trouble," replied Stuart. "She took Vitamin D when she needed A. She took B when she was short of C. Let it be a lesson to all of us!" He glared fiercely at the children and they made no more inquiries about Miss Gunderson.

"Everyone will now take his or her seat!" commanded Stuart. The pupils filed obediently down the aisles and dropped on to their seats, and in a moment there was silence in the classroom. Stuart cleared his throat. Seizing a coat lapel in either hand, to make himself look like a professor, Stuart began:

"Anybody absent?"

The scholars shook their heads.

"Anybody late?"

They shook their heads.

"Very well," said Stuart, "what's the first subject you usually take up in the morning?"

"Arithmetic," shouted the children.

"Bother Arithmetic!" snapped Stuart. "Let's skip it."

There were wild shouts of enthusiasm at this suggestion. Everyone in the class seemed perfectly willing to skip Arithmetic for one morning.

"What next do you study?" asked Stuart.

"Spelling," cried the children.

"Well," said Stuart, "a mis-spelled word is an abomination in the sight of everyone. I consider it a very fine thing to spell words correctly and I strongly urge every one of you to buy a dictionary and consult it whenever you are in the slightest doubt. So much for Spelling. What's next?"

The scholars were just as pleased to be let out of Spelling as they were about Arithmetic, and they shouted for joy, and everybody looked at everybody else and laughed and waved rulers. Stuart had to climb on to the pile of books again and dive for the bell to restore order.

"What's next?" he repeated.

"Writing," cried the scholars.

"Goodness," said Stuart in disgust, "don't you children know how to write yet?"

"Certainly we do!" yelled one and all.

"So much for that, then," said Stuart.

"Social Studies come next," cried Elizabeth Gardner, eagerly.

"Social Studies? Never heard of them," said Stuart. "Instead of taking up any special subject this morning wouldn't it be a good idea if we just talked about something?"

The scholars glanced around at each other in expectancy.

"Could we talk about the way it feels to hold a snake in your hand?" asked Arthur Greenlaw.

"We could, but I'd rather not," replied Stuart.

"Could we talk about the fat woman at the circus?" begged Isidor Feinberg, reminiscently.

"No," said Stuart. "I'll tell you, let's talk about the King of the World." He looked all around the room hopefully to see how the children liked that idea.

$$\frac{5}{8} \times 1\frac{1}{12}$$

$$3$$
$$9000 \quad -$$

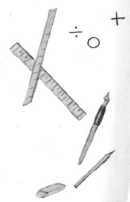

"There isn't any King of the World," said Harry Jamieson in disgust.

"What's the diff?" said Stuart. "There ought to be one."

"Kings are old-fashioned," said Harry.

"Well, all right then, let's talk about the Chairman of the World. The world gets into a lot of trouble because it has no chairman. I would like to be Chairman of the World myself."

"You're too small," said Mary Bendix.

"Oh, fish feathers!" said Stuart. "Size has nothing to do with it. It's ability that counts. The Chairman has to have ability and he must know what's important. How many of you know what's important?"

Up went all the hands.

"Very good," said Stuart, cocking one leg across the other and shoving his hands in the pockets of his jacket. "Henry Rackmeyer, you tell us what is important."

"A shaft of sunlight, a note of music, and the way the back of a baby's neck smells if its mother keeps it nice," answered Henry.

"Correct," said Stuart. "Those are the important things. You forgot one thing, though. Mary Bendix, what did Henry forget?"

"He forgot ice cream with chocolate sauce on it," said Mary quickly.

"Exactly," said Stuart. "Ice cream is important. Well now, if I'm going to be Chairman of the World this morning, we've got to have some rules. We've got to have some laws if we're going to play this game. Can anybody suggest any good laws for the world?"

"Don't eat mushrooms, they might be toadstools," suggested Albert Fernstrom.

"That's not a law," said Stuart, "that's merely a bit of friendly advice. Advice and law are not the same. Law is much more solemn. Anybody else think of a law for the world?"

"Nix on swiping anything," suggested John Poldowski, solemnly.

"Very good," said Stuart. "Good law."

"Never poison anything but rats," said Anthony Brendisi.

"That's no good," said Stuart. "It's unfair to rats. A law has to be fair to everybody."

Anthony looked sulky. "But rats are unfair to us," he said. "Rats are objectionable."

"I know they are," said Stuart. "But from a rat's point of view, poison is objectionable. A Chairman has to see all sides to a problem."

"Have you got a rat's point of view?" asked Anthony. "You look a little like a rat."

"No," replied Stuart, "I have more the point of view of a mouse, which is very different. Any other ideas for laws?"

Agnes Beretska raised her hand. "There ought to be a law against fighting."

"Impractical," said Stuart. "Men like to fight. But you're getting warm, Agnes."

"No scrapping?" asked Agnes, timidly. Stuart shook his head.

"Absolutely no being mean," suggested Mildred Hoffenstein.

"Very fine law," said Stuart. "When I am Chairman, anybody who is mean to anybody else is going to catch it."

"That won't work," remarked Herbert Prendergast. "Some people are just naturally mean. Albert Fernstrom is always being mean to me."

"I'm not saying it'll work," said Stuart. "It's a good law and we'll give it a try. We'll give it a try right here and now. Somebody do something mean to somebody. Harry Jamieson, you be mean to Katharine Stableford. Wait a minute, now, what's that you've got in your hand, Katharine?"

"It's a little tiny lavender bag."

"Do you like it very much?" asked Stuart.

"Yes, I do," said Katharine.

"O.K., Harry, grab it, take it away!"

Harry ran over to where Katharine sat, grabbed the little pillow from her hand, and ran back to his seat, while Katharine screamed.

"Now then," said Stuart in a fierce voice, "hold on while your Chairman consults the book of rules!" He pretended to thumb through a book. "Here we are. Page 492. 'Absolutely no being mean.' Page 560. 'Nix on swiping anything.' Harry Jamieson has broken two laws. Let's get Harry before he becomes so mean, people will hardly recognize him any more! Come on!"

Stuart ran for the pointer and slid down, like a fireman coming down a pole in a fire-station. He ran towards Harry, and the other children jumped up from their seats and crowded around Harry while Stuart demanded that he give up the little pillow. Harry looked frightened, although he knew it was just a test. He gave Katharine the pillow.

"There, it worked pretty well," said Stuart. "No being mean is a perfectly good law." He wiped his face with his handkerchief, for he was quite warm from the exertion of being Chairman of the World. Katharine was very pleased to have her pillow back.

"Let's see that little pillow a minute," said Stuart. Katharine showed it to him. It was about as long as Stuart was high, and Stuart suddenly thought what a fine, sweet-smelling bed it would make for him. He began to want the pillow himself.

"That's a very pretty thing," said Stuart. "You don't want to sell it, do you?"

"Oh, no," replied Katharine. "It was a present to me. Some one gave it to me last summer."

"Ah," said Stuart, "summers are wonderful, aren't they?"

"Yes," said Katharine, "and last summer was the most wonderful summer I have ever had in my whole life."

"I can imagine," replied Stuart, dreamily. "You're sure you wouldn't want to sell that little pillow?"

Katharine shook her head.

"Don't know as I blame you," replied Stuart, quietly. "Summer-time is important. Never forget your summer-times, my dears." He sighed. "Well, I've got to be getting along. It's been a pleasure to know you all. Class is dismissed!"

Stuart strode rapidly to the door, climbed into his car, and with a final wave of the hand drove off in a northerly direction, while the children raced alongside and screamed, "Good-bye, good-bye, good-bye!"

They all wished they could have a Substitute every day, instead of Miss Gunderson.

THROUGH THE FIRE

LITTLE Jack sat alone by the fire. He was seven years old, but so small and pale that he looked little more than five. He had no brothers or sisters, and he was nearly always alone, for his mother, who was a widow, went out all day to teach music, and often in the evening also to play at children's parties. They lived on the third floor of a small house in a dull old street in London in Victorian times. To-night he felt sadder than usual, for it was Christmas Eve, and his mother had gone to a child's party.

"It's a shame," he said, and the tears rose to his eyes. "A dreadful shame. I think it's too bad!" and he seized the poker and gave the fire a great dig.

"For pity's sake, don't do that again," said a small voice from the flames; "it's enough to break one to bits."

Jack stopped crying and looked into the fire. There he saw a little figure, the strangest he had ever beheld, balancing itself skilfully on the top of a piece of burning coal. It was just like a little man, not more than three inches high, dressed from head to foot in orange-scarlet, the colour of flame, and wearing on his head a long pointed cap of the same colour.

"Who are you?" asked Jack.

"I'm a fire-fairy."

"But I don't believe in fairies," said Jack.

The little man laughed. "You'd never have a fire but for us; we light them and keep them in. If I were to go away now, your fire would be out in an instant."

"But how is it you don't get burnt up?" asked Jack.

"Burnt up!" said the little man scornfully; "why, we breathe fire and live in it; we should go out at once if we weren't surrounded by it."

Jack was silent for a little, then he said: "I wonder I never saw you before."

"I have always been there; so it has been only your own stupidity," said the gnome.

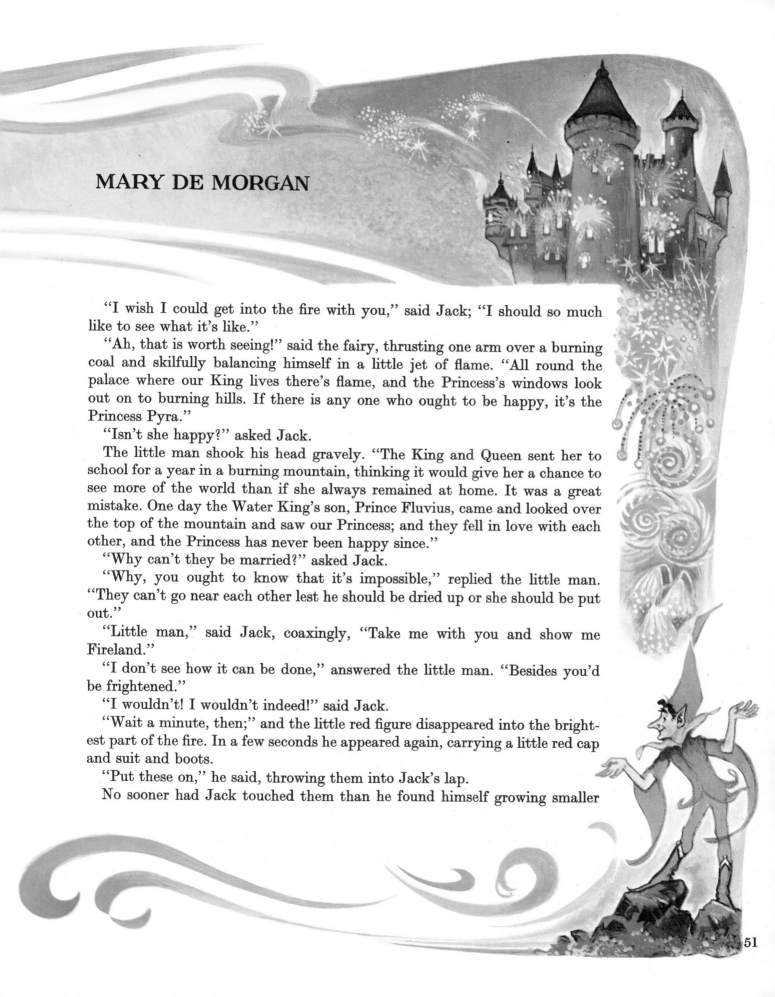

MARY DE MORGAN

"I wish I could get into the fire with you," said Jack; "I should so much like to see what it's like."

"Ah, that is worth seeing!" said the fairy, thrusting one arm over a burning coal and skilfully balancing himself in a little jet of flame. "All round the palace where our King lives there's flame, and the Princess's windows look out on to burning hills. If there is any one who ought to be happy, it's the Princess Pyra."

"Isn't she happy?" asked Jack.

The little man shook his head gravely. "The King and Queen sent her to school for a year in a burning mountain, thinking it would give her a chance to see more of the world than if she always remained at home. It was a great mistake. One day the Water King's son, Prince Fluvius, came and looked over the top of the mountain and saw our Princess; and they fell in love with each other, and the Princess has never been happy since."

"Why can't they be married?" asked Jack.

"Why, you ought to know that it's impossible," replied the little man. "They can't go near each other lest he should be dried up or she should be put out."

"Little man," said Jack, coaxingly, "Take me with you and show me Fireland."

"I don't see how it can be done," answered the little man. "Besides you'd be frightened."

"I wouldn't! I wouldn't indeed!" said Jack.

"Wait a minute, then;" and the little red figure disappeared into the brightest part of the fire. In a few seconds he appeared again, carrying a little red cap and suit and boots.

"Put these on," he said, throwing them into Jack's lap.

No sooner had Jack touched them than he found himself growing smaller

and smaller, until the clothes seemed the right size for him, and he easily slipped into them.

"Now," said the fire-man. "Climb over the bars and see how you like it."

Jack scrambled over the fender, and helping himself with the fire-irons, climbed on to the first bar. The red man leant down and gave him his hand to help him. What a hot hand it was! It burned like flame. Jack scrambled over the bars right into the midst of the fire.

He stood in the middle of rich, red-glowing hills, from which spouted jets of flame, like trees. Here and there was a black mountain which smoked and hissed.

"Well," said the red man, "how do you feel now?"

"It's warm," murmured poor Jack.

"If you can't bear this, you won't be able to stand Fireland," said the fairy.

"I daresay soon I shall feel quite used to it," said Jack, making an effort. "How does one get to Fireland?"

"I'll show you," said the little man, and dug into the coal beneath his feet till he had made a good-sized hole. Then he took from his pocket some little marbles, and dropped them one by one into the hole which gradually began to grow larger and larger until it was an immense black gulf.

"Now come along," said the red man, sitting on the edge with his legs swinging over. "Get on to my shoulders and put your legs round my neck. Give me your hands, and I'll take you quite safely."

Jack did as he was told, and they went down—down—down. It was pitch dark. At last he saw a faint red light growing larger and brighter every moment. "There's Fireland," said his guide.

As they passed from the darkness into the light through a kind of archway, Jack looked about him. There were great hills, and they were every shade of red and orange, some pale, some bright, and on the hillsides were lakes of fire. The sky was one mass of flame. On they went until they came in sight of a large city with tall spires and bridges, and a little way out of it stood a palace made of red-hot iron and glistening with precious stones.

"That's the King's palace," said the fire-man. "We'll go there first."

"Shall I see the Princess?" asked Jack eagerly.

"Most likely she'll be in the palace garden."

They stopped in front of the gate, and the fire-fairy told Jack he could go in.

It was the queerest palace and garden. Jack now saw that what he had at first supposed to be precious stones were nothing but different coloured fires, spouting out all over the palace. There was blue fire, and red fire, and green fire, and yellow fire, shining against the palace walls just like jewels.

At first Jack thought that the garden was full of beautiful flowers, but when he drew near he saw that they were fireworks in the forms of flowers. There was every sort of catherine-wheel turning round as fast as possible, throwing off sparks; and every now and then a brilliant rocket went up into the air and fell in shining stars.

A group of ladies came slowly down the path. In their midst walked the Princess. Her long, bright, golden hair fell almost to her feet. Her face was very pale with a very sad expression. She wore a shining, flame-coloured dress with a long train, and one pale blue and silver catherine-wheel fixed in her hair.

Jack, seeing her so unhappy, burst out:

"Oh, poor Princess!"

At this the Princess raised her eyes—such bright eyes they were, shining just like stars.

"Who spoke?" said the Princess in a low, sad voice.

Despite the red fire-man, who did his best to hold him back, Jack stepped in front of the Princess and said:

"If you please, your Royal Highness, I did."

"And who are you?" asked the Princess kindly.

"I'm a little boy, and my name is Jack."

"How did you come here?"

"I came with him," said Jack, pointing to the red fire-man. "Please don't be angry with him."

"I am not in the least angry," said the Princess. "But I want to know why you pity me."

"I think it's very sad for you to be parted from your Prince," said Jack.

Here all the ladies crowded round him and tried to stop him speaking, but the Princess said:

"Silence! It does no harm for me to hear him." And just as the Princess spoke, a cloud of smoke was seen rolling over the hills and the ladies cried:

"The King! The King!"

"Go! Go!" cried the Princess to Jack; and the fire-man, without more ado, seized him, and placing him on his shoulders flew through the air with him at a great rate, and was far from the palace before Jack could get breath to speak.

"A fine mess you nearly got me into!" grumbled the little man. "What would have happened to me if the King had come up and heard you talking to the Princess of the very subject he had forbidden us all to mention?"

Jack dared not say a word as his companion was so angry and on they went at a dreadful pace until they reached the long dark tunnel, and when they again came towards the light, the little man took Jack from his shoulders and flung him away with all his force, and he remembered nothing more till he found himself lying on the hearth-rug in his own room. The fire had gone out and the only light in the room came from the street-lamps. Jack jumped up and searched everywhere for any trace of the little man but could fine none. He ran to the fireplace and called, but there was no answer, and at last he went shivering and cold to bed to dream of the Princess and the strange bright country underground.

*   *   *   *

New Year's Eve came, and again Jack's mother had to go and leave him. It was raining and the wind blew in great melancholy gusts. Jack sat by the window and looked out on the wet street and the driving clouds.

"Little Jack!" called a low, sighing voice from the grate.

Jack started, and ran to the fireplace. The fire was almost out. There was only a dull red glare in the coals, but kneeling in it, holding on to the bars, was the Fire Princess. She was paler than before and looked quite transparent. Jack could see the coals plainly through her.

"Put on some more coal," she said, shivering. "There is not enough for me to burn here, and if you don't keep a good blaze I shall go out altogether."

Jack mended the fire, then sat down on the hearth-rug and stared at the Princess. Her long, bright hair fell over the bars, and though her face looked very small and pale, her eyes were immense, and glittered like diamonds.

"I want you to do me a favour," she said.

"What is it?" asked Jack.

"Let the Prince come here and speak to me."

"How am I to bring him?"

"I will show you. Is it raining to-night?"

"Yes, fast."

"That is very lucky; some of his people are sure to be about. Then all you must do is open the window and wait."

So Jack threw open one of the windows. A great gust of wind blew into the room and blew the cold wet rain into his face.

"Now, little Jack, look on the window-sill."

Just outside, seated on the sill in a little pool of water, was a tiny man dressed in dull green. He had long wavy hair that looked heavy and wet, and his clothes were shiny with water.

"Tell him," whispered the Princess, "that he must bring Prince Fluvius here;" and Jack repeated her message to the water-fairy. The water-fairy at once disappeared. Suddenly the room began to grow dark.

"He is coming," said the Princess.

Then there floated up outside the window a white cloud which rested on the sill. The cloud opened, and from it stepped the figure of a young man, gorgeously dressed in silver and green. His eyes were a deep blue, just the colour of the sea.

At sight of Princess Pyra, he would have dashed right up to the bars, had she not begged him, for both their sakes, not to come inside the window.

"At least we should perish together," sighed the Prince.

"No," said the Princess. "Since I last saw you I have learned that there is only one person in the world who can help us, and that is the old man at the North Pole."

"But how are we to send to him?" said the Prince. "If you were to go, the sea would surely quench you, and I should be frozen. As for the wind-fairies, they are such silly little things they could never remember a message."

"Little Jack," cried the Princess, "you will go for us, will you not?"

"I?" cried Jack in alarm. He looked at the Prince sitting on the window-sill, then at the Princess kneeling on the glowing coals, and they both looked so sad that he could not bear to refuse.

"Then it is settled," said the Princess, smiling. "Listen very carefully. The old man at the North Pole is very cunning and of one thing you must be very careful. You must not ask him more than one question. The first question he is asked he is bound to answer truthfully, but if you ask him more than one, he will at once seize you and keep you under the ice. Say, '*I come from the Fire Princess Pyra, and she is in love with Prince Fluvius, the Water Prince, and wants to know how they are to be married*;' and then shut your lips and do not speak again. Go to the window and you will see the wind-fairy who is to take you."

There stood a little man dressed in light dust-coloured clothes which hung on him loosely, and whenever he moved there came a violent gust of wind.

"Sit on his shoulders," said Prince Fluvius, "and he will take you quite safely," and he touched Jack lightly on the top of his head.

Jack felt himself growing smaller and smaller.

"Come on, then," said the wind-fairy in an odd gusty voice and off they went, the rain beating into Jack's face as they flew over the tops of the houses and among the chimney-pots. He held on tightly to the wind-fairy's neck, and at last they came in sight of the sea.

"I hope I shan't tumble in," said Jack.

"I shall keep tight hold of you," replied the wind-fairy.

The sea danced and sparkled beneath them.

On they went, and it began to grow very cold. "We had better stop here," said the wind-fairy, placing Jack on a great lump of floating ice. "I will get out the fire-ball which the Princess gave me to keep you warm."

"See," said the wind-fairy, taking up Jack again, "I have sent the fire-ball on before us. Now we are in the ice-world. That is the North Pole and you can see the light from the old man's lantern. Now say what you have to say to him quickly, and then I'll take you back."

It was such a strange scene! The little old man nursed his knees with his arms and hugged a huge lantern. He wore a big brown cloak, and on his head a small skull-cap, from beneath which fell his long straight white hair. He was a very ugly old man; there was no doubt about that. He seemed to be asleep, for his head hung over on one side and his eyes were shut. He might have remained so for ever if the wind-fairy had not blown a tremendous gust which made the pink light in the lantern flicker and the old man start up and open his eyes.

"Who are you?" he asked. "Come to ask a question, eh? What is it? What do you want? Speak out!"

Jack tried to remember what the Princess had told him to say.

"I'm come from the Fire Princess, and she wants to marry the Water King's son, and they're afraid of touching each other, lest he should dry up, or she be put out. So please, they want to know what to do."

Jack stopped because the old man was shaking so with laughter that he feared he would tumble off the Pole altogether.

"Oh, the stupidity of people! And all this time they are afraid of doing the very thing they ought to do. Of course it's impossible for them to marry till he is dried up and she is put out. *What puts out fire but water? What dries up water but fire?*—You had better go back to Prince Fluvius and tell him to give her a kiss. Now what do you want to ask next? Let it be something for yourself this time."

A dozen questions flashed into Jack's mind at once, but he remembered the Princess's warning and held his tongue.

"Come, now," said the old man coaxingly; "you'll never go back after asking only one question!" and the old man caught his wrist and held him firmly. But Jack gave a violent wriggle which knocked over the old man's lantern. It fell with a crash which brought the wind-fairy to Jack's side in an instant. He took Jack on his shoulders and flew off with him without a word.

"The fire-ball is gone out," he said to Jack after they had gone a little way. "If you feel sleepy you may as well go to sleep."

Jack did fall into a doze, although he woke every now and then to ask if they were getting near home. At last the fairy said: "Now we are over London."

"I hope my mother isn't come home yet," said Jack. "She'd be so frightened if she came back and didn't find me."

"Why, it isn't twelve o'clock yet," laughed the fairy, "and the New Year is not come in. Here is the street where you live."

From outside, Jack could see the Prince waiting on the window-sill, and when the wind-fairy left him in the middle of the room, there was the Princess with her golden hair falling over the bars of the grate.

"Well," they cried together, "what did he say, little Jack?"

Jack repeated carefully what the old man had said: " '*What puts out fire but water? What dries up water but fire?* Tell him to give her a kiss!' "

"It is as I thought," said the Prince, with a sigh. "He means that there is no hope for us, and that we must perish together."

"Why, no," cried the Princess, "I think now I begin to understand him."

And she stepped lightly from the grate on to the floor, in a halo of shining flame. In the same moment the Prince swept down from the window and a flood of water splashed on to the floor. Without a word, the two rushed into each other's arms.

The room seemed to be filled with a thick mist through which Jack could see nothing; then as it slowly cleared away, he heard the soft voice of the Princess. She was no longer surrounded by flames, and the weird brightness had passed from her face and dress. Her eyes no longer seemed to burn or her hair to glitter. Beside her stood Prince Fluvius, no less changed. His eyes were bright and his hair had lost its wet gloss.

At that moment, the clock began to strike twelve and all the bells in the great city rang out to tell the world that the New Year was born. As they rang, the room was filled with the strangest forms. Fairies, goblins, elves, floated in at the open window and pressed around the Prince and Princess, filling every nook and corner of the room. With every stroke of the clock, with every clash of the bells, their number increased, but at the sixth stroke, the young couple moved towards the window.

"Good-bye, little Jack; we shall never forget you!" called the Princess.

"Good-bye, little Jack," echoed the Prince; "we shall come if ever you want us!" And at the last stroke of twelve, they were gone. The room was left empty and cold, and little Jack was alone.

*   *   *   *

A whole year had passed and Jack had seen nothing of his fairy friends. Christmas had come round again, but this was a very different Christmas for little Jack was very ill. Christmas week passed, and New Year's Eve came, and still Jack lay in bed. "This time last year I saw the Princess," he sighed.

"Little Jack!" called a low, sweet voice, and there at the window, standing in a moonbeam, were the Prince and Princess.

"Now see what we have brought you," said the Princess. "This is a magic belt. You must put it on and it will make you strong again. No one will know it is there, for directly it is upon you it will become invisible."

The Prince and Princess slipped the belt over Jack's head and fastened it round his waist, but when it was on he could neither feel nor see it.

"Farewell, dear little Jack," they said. "This time we part for ever." Then both Prince and Princess floated up on the moonbeam.

From the very next day Jack began to get well, but when he told his mother about the Princess and the wonderful belt he wore, she only shook her head and said with a smile: "Dear boy, you have had a dream. I am glad it was such a pleasant one."

Years afterwards, he often felt for the belt but never could find it, but when his mother rejoiced that he had grown to be such a tall, strong boy, he smiled to himself and said: "It all came of my going to the North Pole for the Fire Princess."

The WATCHMAKER'S SHOP

A street in our town
    Has a queer little shop
With tumble-down walls
    And a thatch on the top;
And all the wee windows
    With crookedy panes
Are shining and winking
    With watches and chains.

(All sorts and sizes
    In silver and gold,
And brass ones and tin ones
    And new ones and old;
And clocks for the kitchen
    And clocks for the hall,
High ones and low ones
    And wag-at-the-wall.)

The watchmaker sits
  On a long-leggèd seat
And bids you the time
  Of the day when you meet;
And round and about him
  There's ticketty-tock
From the tiniest watch
  To the grandfather clock.

I wonder he doesn't
  Get tired of the chime
And all the clocks ticking
  And telling the time;
But there he goes winding
  Lest any should stop,
This queer little man
  In the watchmaker's shop.

A DAY ON THE ALM

JOHANNA SPYRI

EARLY in the morning, Heidi was awakened by a loud whistle. As she opened her eyes, a gleam of sunshine came through the little window on to her bed and shone on the hay nearby so that everything was bathed in golden light. Heidi looked puzzled and tried to think where she was. Then, from outside, she heard the grandfather's deep, quiet voice and she remembered that she was up on the Alm. She no longer lived with old Ursel who was almost stone deaf and always wanted to have Heidi by her side, so that sometimes the child had felt like a prisoner and would have liked to run away. So she was very glad when she awoke and found herself in her new home. She remembered all the exciting things she had seen the previous day and wondered what this new day had in store for her. Above all she looked forward to seeing the goats, Little Swan and Little Bear, again. Quickly she jumped out of bed and in a few minutes had dressed herself. Then she climbed down the steps and ran out to the front of the cottage. Peter, the goat-herd, was already there with his flock and the grandfather was leading out Little Swan and Little Bear to join them. Heidi ran forward to say good morning to him and the goats.

"How would you like to go with them to the pasture?" asked the grandfather.

Heidi was overjoyed. That was the thing she would like best of all.

"But first you must wash yourself or the sun, shining brightly up there, will laugh at you when he looks down and sees how dirty you are! See! This is where you wash." The grandfather pointed towards a big flat tub filled with water which stood in the sun before the cottage door. Heidi jumped towards it and splashed and scrubbed until she was perfectly clean. In the meantime, the grandfather went into the cottage, calling to Peter, "Come here, goat-general, and bring your rucksack!"

Amazed, Peter answered the call and laid down the rucksack in which he carried his meagre lunch.

"Open it!" ordered the old man, and then put in a big piece of bread and an equally big piece of cheese. Peter opened his round eyes very wide for this food was twice as much as he had for his own lunch.

"And now the little bowl has to go in," the old man continued. "At lunch-time you will milk for her two little bowlfuls, for she is going, too, and can stay with you until you come back in the evening. Take care she doesn't fall over the precipice!"

Now Heidi came running towards them. "Grandfather, the sun can't laugh at me now!" For fear of the sun's mockery she had rubbed her face, neck and arms so vigorously with the rough cloth which the grandfather had hung up beside the water-tub, that she was almost as red as a lobster.

The old man smiled. "No, he has no reason to laugh now," he agreed. "But do you know what happens when you come home in the evening? You go right into the tub like a fish because if you run like the goats your feet will get dirty. Now, off you go!"

Happily the children climbed up the Alm. The high winds during the night had blown away the last little cloud and now the sky was a vast expanse of deep blue out of which the sun shone and glittered on the green slopes. The little blue and yellow mountain flowers opened their cups and seemed to nod merrily at Heidi who romped everywhere. Enchanted by this sparkling, waving sea of flowers, she forgot all about Peter, even about the goats. All along the way she picked flowers until she had a big bunch which she wrapped in her pinafore, for she wanted to take them home.

Peter was quite dazed trying to look in every direction at once, for the goats, like Heidi, were jumping from one place to another. He had to whistle and shout and brandish his stick to bring the goats together again.

"Where are you now, Heidi?" came the boy's exasperated and rather angry cry.

"Here!" came the reply, but Peter could see no one. Heidi was sitting, hidden from view, behind a little hillock.

"Come here!" Peter called again. "You are not to go near the precipice the uncle said so!"

"Where is that?" asked Heidi, still not moving from her hiding-place.

"Up there! Right on the top the old eagle sits on the look-out for his prey." That did the trick.

At once Heidi jumped up and ran to Peter with her apronful of flowers.

"That is enough flower-picking for now," he said as they climbed up together, "if you are going to keep pace with me. And if you pick all the flowers to-day there will be none left for to-morrow."

Heidi was convinced. Moreover, her pinafore was so full that it could hardly hold another one. So she now walked quietly beside Peter. The pasture which

Peter usually chose and where he spent the day was situated at the foot of the high rocks. Bushes and fir trees covered the lower parts but nearer the summit the rocks rose bare and rugged towards the sky. On one side of the mountain, jagged clefts stretched far down and the grandfather had been right to warn Peter of the danger. When they had reached the pasture, Peter carefully put his rucksack into a little hollow in the ground, for the wind often blew with great violence across this part of the country and Peter did not want to see his precious possessions rolling down the mountainside. Then the boy, tired after the strenuous climb, stretched himself out at full length on the sunny pasture.

Heidi, by this time, had undone her pinafore and rolled it neatly round the flowers which she laid beside Peter's rucksack in the hollow. Then she sat down beside him and looked around. The valley lay far below, bathed in the sparkling morning sunshine. In front of Heidi a big, broad snowfield rose up to the dark blue sky and on the left stood a huge pile of rocks above which a bare rocky peak reached towards the sky, towering majestically above the child. Heidi sat motionless. A great silence was all around and only the delicate blue hare-bells and yellow cistus swayed softly in the gentle breeze, nodding joyfully on their slender little stems. Peter had fallen asleep and the goats were climbing high up amongst the bushes. Heidi had never been so happy. The golden sunlight, the fresh breezes and the delicate perfume of the flowers filled her with delight and she only wished that she might stay there for ever. She gazed so long at the mountains that it seemed to her that each had a face and that these mountain-faces were as familiar to her as old friends.

Suddenly Heidi heard a loud, harsh cry and when she looked up she saw, circling overhead, a huge bird, larger than she had ever seen before. His wings were outspread and he flew in a wide circle, coming back again and again and uttering loud, piercing shrieks above Heidi's head.

"Peter! Peter! Wake up!" cried Heidi, "Look! There is a big bird just above us!"

Peter got up and watched the bird, too, as it rose higher and higher and at last disappeared behind the grey rocks.

"Where has he gone to?" asked Heidi who had been watching the bird with keen interest.

"Home to his nest," replied Peter.

"Is his home up there? Oh, how nice to live so high up! How terribly he cries! Let's climb up there and see where his nest is!"

"Oh, no!" replied Peter emphatically. "Even the goats can't climb so high and the uncle said you were not to climb the rocks."

Suddenly Peter started to whistle and call loudly. Heidi could not think what this meant, but the goats apparently understood, for, one after another, they came springing down until they were all gathered together on the green slope. Some continued to nibble and others ran about, playfully pushing each other with their horns. Heidi jumped up and ran amongst them. While she played with the goats Peter fetched the rucksack and laid out the four pieces of bread on the ground, the big ones on Heidi's side and the small ones on his own. Then he took the little bowl, drew some milk into it from Little Swan and placed it in the centre. "Stop skipping now! It is time to eat," he said.

Heidi sat down. "Is the milk for me?" she asked.

"Yes," replied Peter, "and the two big pieces of bread and cheese are yours too, and when you have finished you get another bowlful from Little Swan."

Heidi began to drink her milk and as soon as she put down her empty bowl Peter filled it again. Then Heidi gave a big piece of her bread to Peter and all the cheese as well, saying, "You can have it all. I have had enough."

Peter gazed at her, speechless with surprise. Never in his life could he have given away as much as that. He hesitated a little, for he could not believe that Heidi meant it seriously. She held out the pieces, but as Peter still did not take them she laid the food on his knees. Peter had never before had such a satisfying lunch.

The animals had begun to climb up again towards the bushes; some skipping gaily over everything, others stopping to taste the tender herbs.

"Peter," Heidi said presently, "the prettiest of all are Little Swan and Little Bear."

"I know," Peter replied. "The uncle brushes and washes them, and gives them salt, and has the nicest shed."

Suddenly Peter jumped up and bounded after the goats. Heidi followed. Something must have happened and she simply could not stay behind. Peter forced his way through the middle of the herd to that side of the Alm where the bare and jagged rocks fell away steeply. Here, a heedless little goat might easily tumble down and break his legs. Peter had noticed inquisitive little Goldfinch jumping in that direction. The boy arrived just in time, for the little goat was just about to jump towards the edge of the precipice. Peter, lunging towards the goat fell down and only managed to seize one of its legs as he fell. Goldfinch gave an angry cry at finding herself caught and tried desperately to free herself. Peter could not get up and shouted for Heidi to help because he was afraid Goldfinch might wrench her leg. Heidi was already there and at once saw the danger. She quickly gathered some sweet-smelling plants from the ground and held them out towards Goldfinch, saying coaxingly, "Come along, Goldfinch, and be good! Look! You might fall down and hurt yourself."

The little goat turned quickly and ate the herbs from Heidi's outstretched hand. In the meantime Peter got to his feet again and held Goldfinch by the cord with which her little bell was fastened to her neck. Heidi grasped the goat in the same way at the other side of its head and together they led the truant back to the peacefully grazing flock. As soon as Peter got her back to safety, he raised his stick and started to give her a good beating. Goldfinch, however, knowing what was in store, timidly shrank back, and Heidi cried, "No, Peter! No! You mustn't beat her! Look how frightened she is!"

"She deserves it," Peter muttered, about to strike; but Heidi threw herself against his arm, crying indignantly, "Don't touch her! You will hurt her! Leave her alone!"

Peter turned surprised eyes on the fierce little girl and his stick dropped to his side. "All right, then, I'll let her off—if you give me some of your cheese to-morrow again," he bargained.

"You can have it all, to-morrow and every day. I don't want it," Heidi consented. "And I'll give you the bread, too, the same as to-day, but you must promise never to beat Goldfinch or Snowflake, or any of the goats."

"Suits me," said Peter, and that was as good as a promise. He let Goldfinch go and the little goat leapt joyously towards the herd.

So the day passed quickly and the sun began to sink behind the mountains. Heidi was sitting quietly on the ground, gazing at the cistus and the harebells which glistened in the evening sunshine; rocks and grass shimmered in a golden glow. Suddenly she jumped up and cried, "Peter! Peter! They are on fire! They are all on fire! All the mountains are burning! And the great snow mountain also, and the sky! Oh, look at the lovely fiery snow! Peter, get up and look! The fire is at the great bird's nest, too. Look at the rocks and the fir trees! Everything is on fire!"

"It is always like that," replied Peter with great unconcern, "but it is not real fire."

"What is it, then?" asked Heidi, gazing eagerly around. "What is it, Peter?"

"It just gets like that," Peter tried to explain.

"Oh, look, Peter!" cried Heidi again in great excitement. "Everything is turning a rosy pink colour. Look at the snow and the high rocks! What are their names, Peter?"

"Mountains don't have names," replied Peter.

"Oh, how beautiful! Crimson snow! Oh, now all the rocks are turning grey— now the colour is all gone. Now it is all over, Peter."

Heidi sat down, looking as distressed as if everything really had come to an end.

"To-morrow it will be the same," said Peter. "Get up now. We must go home."

"Will it be like this every day we are on the pasture?" asked Heidi insistently, as she walked down the Alm at Peter's side.

"Mostly," he replied.

Heidi was very happy. She had absorbed so many new impressions—had so many new things to think about that she was quite silent until they reached the hut and saw the grandfather sitting on the bench under the fir trees. Here he sat in the evenings, waiting for his goats.

Heidi ran up to him, followed by Little Swan and Little Bear, for the goats knew their master.

"Good night!" Peter called after Heidi, and then added, "Come again, to-morrow!" because he was very anxious for her to go with him.

Heidi raced towards the old man.

"Oh, Grandfather, it was wonderful!" she cried long before she reached him. "The fire on the snow and the rocks and the blue and yellow flowers, and look what I have brought for you!" Heidi unfolded her pinafore and all the flowers fell at the grandfather's feet. But what a sight the poor flowers were! Heidi did not recognise them. They were like withered grass and not a single little cup was open. "Grandfather, what is the matter with the flowers?" cried Heidi, quite alarmed. "They weren't like that before. What is wrong with them?"

"They would rather be out in the sun than tied up in a pinafore," explained the grandfather.

"Then I will never gather any more. But Grandfather, why did the eagle screech so?" Heidi asked.

"You had better have your bath now," said the grandfather, "and I shall fetch some milk from the shed. Afterwards, when we are having our supper you can tell me about everything."

Later, when Heidi sat in her high chair, the little bowl of milk in front of her and the grandfather at her side, she again asked her question.

"Why did the great bird scream at us, Grandfather?"

"He screams in mockery of the people in the villages down in the valley where they sit gossiping together. He wants to say, 'If you would all mind your own business or climb up into the heights like me you would be much happier!'"

The grandfather spoke these words with such vehemence that Heidi seemed to hear again the croaking of the great bird.

"Why don't the mountains have names, Grandfather?" asked Heidi again.

"They have names," he answered, "and if you can describe one to me so that I can recognise it, then I will tell you its name."

Heidi tried to describe the rocky mountain with the two high peaks exactly as she had seen it. Presently the grandfather interrupted, "Yes, I know that one. Its name is Falknis. Did you notice any others?"

Then Heidi recalled the mountain with the large snowfield which looked at first as if it were on fire and then turned rose-coloured, then pale pink, and at last faded back to its own grey colour.

"I know that one, too," said the grandfather. "That is the Scesaplana. Did you like being on the pasture?"

Now Heidi told him everything: how wonderful it had been and particularly about the fire in the evening. Heidi wanted the grandfather to explain why this had happened, since Peter had been unable to do so.

"You see," the grandfather instructed her, "that's what the sun does when he says good night to the mountains. He throws his most beautiful rays over them so that they won't forget him before morning."

Heidi was delighted. She could hardly wait for the next day when she would again be allowed to go to the pasture, to watch how the sun said good night to the mountains. But first she had to go to bed, and how soundly she slept all night on her hay bed and dreamt of nothing but glistening mountains tinged with red, and Little Snowflake running happily about!

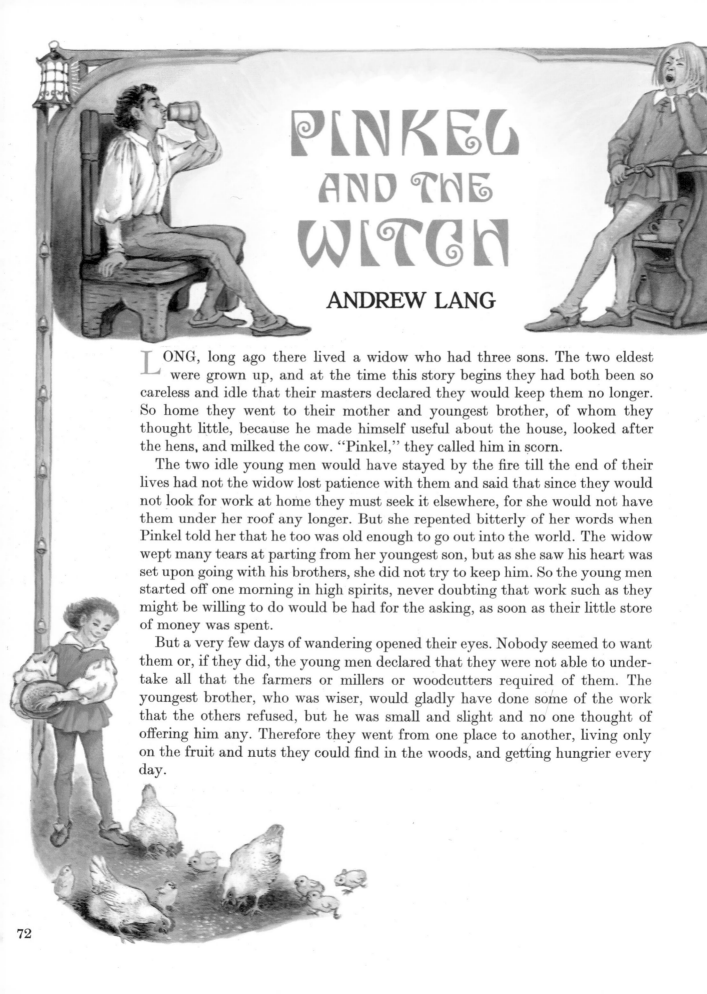

PINKEL AND THE WITCH

ANDREW LANG

L ONG, long ago there lived a widow who had three sons. The two eldest were grown up, and at the time this story begins they had both been so careless and idle that their masters declared they would keep them no longer. So home they went to their mother and youngest brother, of whom they thought little, because he made himself useful about the house, looked after the hens, and milked the cow. "Pinkel," they called him in scorn.

The two idle young men would have stayed by the fire till the end of their lives had not the widow lost patience with them and said that since they would not look for work at home they must seek it elsewhere, for she would not have them under her roof any longer. But she repented bitterly of her words when Pinkel told her that he too was old enough to go out into the world. The widow wept many tears at parting from her youngest son, but as she saw his heart was set upon going with his brothers, she did not try to keep him. So the young men started off one morning in high spirits, never doubting that work such as they might be willing to do would be had for the asking, as soon as their little store of money was spent.

But a very few days of wandering opened their eyes. Nobody seemed to want them or, if they did, the young men declared that they were not able to undertake all that the farmers or millers or woodcutters required of them. The youngest brother, who was wiser, would gladly have done some of the work that the others refused, but he was small and slight and no one thought of offering him any. Therefore they went from one place to another, living only on the fruit and nuts they could find in the woods, and getting hungrier every day.

One night, after they had been walking for many hours and were very tired, they came to a large lake with an island in the middle of it. From the island streamed a strong light, by which they could see everything almost as clearly as if the sun had been shining, and they perceived a boat lying half hidden in the rushes.

"Let us take it and row over to the island, where there must be a house," said the eldest brother; "perhaps they will give us food and shelter."

They all got in the boat and rowed across. As they drew near the island they saw that the light came from a golden lantern hanging over the door of a hut, while sweet tinkling music proceeded from some bells attached to the golden horns of a goat which was feeding near the cottage.

The young men's hearts rejoiced as they thought that at last they would be able to rest their weary limbs and they entered the hut. But they were amazed to see an ugly old woman inside, wrapped in a cloak of gold, which lighted up the whole house. They looked at each other uneasily as she came forward with her daughter, for they knew by the cloak that this was a famous witch.

"What do you want?" asked she, at the same time signing to her daughter to stir the large pot on the fire.

"We are tired and hungry and would fain have shelter for the night," answered the eldest brother.

"You cannot get it here," said the witch, "but you will find both food and shelter in the palace on the other side of the lake. Take your boat and go, but leave this boy with me—I can find work for him, though something tells me he is quick and cunning and will do me ill."

"What harm can a poor boy like me do a great troll like you?" answered Pinkel. "Let me go, I pray you, with my brothers."

At last the witch let him go, and he followed his brothers to the boat.

73

The way was farther than they thought, and it was morning before they reached the palace.

Now, at last, their luck seemed to have turned, for while the two eldest were given places in the King's stables, Pinkel was taken as page to the little prince. Pinkel was a clever and amusing boy, who saw everything that passed under his eyes, and the King noticed this, and often employed him in his own service, which made his brothers very jealous.

Things went on in this way for some time, and every day Pinkel rose in the royal favour. At length the envy of his brothers became so great they could bear it no longer. They did not wish to kill him but merely wished to remind him that he was after all only a child, not half as old and wise as they.

Their opportunity soon came. It happened to be the King's custom to visit his stables once a week to see if the horses were being properly cared for. The next time he entered the stables the two brothers managed to be in the way, and when the King praised the beautiful satin skins of the horses under their charge and remarked how different was their condition when his grooms had first come across the lake, the young men at once began to speak of the wonderful light which sprang from the lantern over the hut. The King, who had a passion for collecting all the rarest things he could find, fell into the trap and inquired where he could get this marvellous lantern.

"Send Pinkel for it, sire," said they. "It belongs to an old witch who no doubt came by it in some evil way. But Pinkel has a smooth tongue and he can get the better of any woman, old or young."

"Then bid him go this very night!" cried the King. "If he brings me the lantern I will make him one of the chief men about my person."

Pinkel was much pleased at the thought of his adventure and, without more ado, he borrowed a little boat which lay moored to the shore and rowed over to the island at once. It was late by the time he arrived and almost dark, but he knew by the savoury smell that reached him the witch was cooking her supper. So he climbed softly on to the roof and, peering down, watched till the old woman's back was turned, when he quickly drew a handful of salt from his pocket and threw it into the pot.

Scarely had he done this when the witch called her daughter and bade her lift the pot off the fire and put the stew into a dish, as it had been cooking quite long enough and she was hungry. But no sooner had she tasted it than she put her spoon down and declared that her daughter must have been meddling with it, for it was impossible to eat anything that was all made of salt.

"Go down to the spring in the valley and get some fresh water that I may prepare a fresh supper," cried she, "for I feel half-starved."

"But, mother," answered the girl, "how can I find the well in the darkness? You know that the lantern's rays shed no light down there."

"Well, then, take the lantern with you," answered the witch, "for supper I must have."

So the girl took her pail in one hand and the golden lantern in the other, and
hastened away to the well, followed by Pinkel, who took care to keep out of
the way of the rays of light. When at last she stooped to fill her pail at the well,
Pinkel snatched up the lantern, hurried back to his boat and rowed off from
the shore.

He was already a long distance from the island when the witch, who wondered
what had become of her daughter, went to the door to look for her. Close around
the hut was thick darkness, but what was that bobbing light that streamed
across the water? The witch's heart sank as it flashed upon her what had
happened.

"Is that you, Pinkel?" cried she.

The youth answered, "Yes, dear mother, it is I!"

"And are you not a knave for robbing me?" said she.

"Truly, dear mother, I am," replied Pinkel rowing faster than ever, for he
was afraid that the witch might come after him.

But she had no power on the water, and turned angrily into the hut, mutter-
ing to herself all the while: "Take care! Take care! A second time you will not
escape so easily!"

The sun had not risen when Pinkel returned to the palace. Entering the
King's chamber, he held up the lantern so that its rays might fall upon the bed.
In an instant the King awoke and seeing the golden lantern shedding its light
upon him, sprang up and embraced Pinkel with joy.

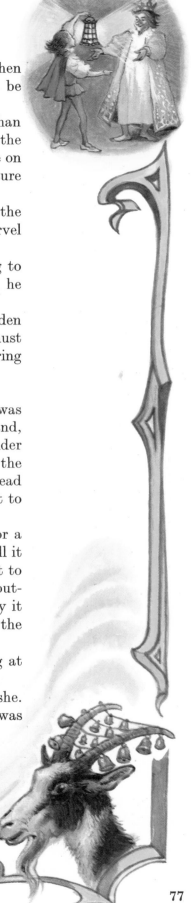

"Oh, cunning one," cried he, "what treasure you have brought me!" Then calling for his attendants he ordered that rooms next to his own should be prepared for Pinkel.

It may easily be guessed that this made the brothers more envious than before. At length they remembered the goat with the golden horns and the bells, and they rejoiced. "For," said they, "this time the old woman will be on the watch, and let him be as clever as he likes, the bells on the horns are sure to warn her."

So when, as before, the King came down to the stables and praised the cleverness of their brother, the young men told him of that other marvel possessed by the witch, the goat with the golden horns.

From this moment the King never closed his eyes at night for longing to possess this wonderful creature and at last, as the brothers had foreseen, he sent for Pinkel.

"I hear," he said, "that the old witch on the island has a goat with golden horns, from which hang bells that tinkle the sweetest music. That goat I must have! I would give the third part of my kingdom to anyone who would bring it to me."

"I will fetch it myself," answered Pinkel.

This time it was easier for Pinkel to approach the island unseen, as there was no golden lantern to throw its beams over the water. But, on the other hand, the goat slept inside the hut and would therefore have to be taken from under the very eyes of the old woman. How was he to do it? All the way across the lake Pinkel thought and thought, till at length a plan came into his head which seemed as if it might do, though he knew it would be very difficult to carry out.

The first thing he did when he reached the shore was to look about for a piece of wood, and when he had found it he hid himself close to the hut till it grew quite dark and near the hour when the witch and her daughter went to bed. Then he crept up and fixed the wood under the door, which opened outward, in such a manner that the more you tried to shut it the more firmly it stuck. And this was what happened when the girl went as usual to bolt the door and make all fast for the night.

"What are you doing?" asked the witch, as her daughter kept tugging at the handle.

"There is something the matter with the door. It won't shut," answered she.

"Well, leave it alone; there is nobody to hurt us," said the witch who was very sleepy; and the girl did as she was bid and went to bed.

Very soon they both were heard snoring, and Pinkel knew that his time was come. Slipping off his shoes he stole into the hut on tiptoe, and taking from his pockets some food of which the goat was particularly fond he laid it under his nose. Then, while the animal was eating it, he stuffed each golden bell with wool which he had also brought with him, stopping every minute to listen, lest the witch should awaken, and he should find himself changed into some dreadful bird or beast. But the snorings still continued, and he went on with his work as quickly as he could.

When the last bell was muffled he drew another handful of food out of his pocket and held it out to the goat, which instantly rose to its feet and followed Pinkel, who backed slowly to the door. Directly he was outside he seized the goat in his arms and ran down to the place where he had moored his boat.

As soon as he had reached the middle of the lake, Pinkel took the wool out of the bells, which began to tinkle loudly. Their sound awoke the witch, who cried out as before:

"Is that you, Pinkel?"

"Yes, dear mother, it is I," said Pinkel.

"Have you stolen my golden goat?" asked she.

"Yes, dear mother, I have," answered Pinkel.

"Are you not a knave, Pinkel?"

"Yes, dear mother, I am," he replied.

And the old witch shouted in a rage, "Ah! Beware how you come hither again, for next time you shall not escape me!"

But Pinkel only laughed and rowed on.

The King was delighted with the goat and as he had promised, Pinkel was made ruler over the third part of the kingdom. As may be supposed, the brothers were more furious than ever and grew quite thin with rage.

"How can we get rid of him?" said one to the other.

And at length they remembered the golden cloak.

"He will need to be clever if he is to take that!" they cried. And when next the King came to see his horses they began to speak of Pinkel and his marvellous cunning, and how he had contrived to get the lantern and the goat which nobody else would have been able to do.

"But as he was there, it is a pity he could not have brought away the golden cloak," added they.

"The golden cloak! What is that?" asked the King.

And the young men described its beauties in such glowing words that the King declared he should never know a day's happiness till he had wrapped the cloak round his own shoulders.

"And," added he, "the man who brings it to me shall wed my daughter and shall inherit my throne."

"None can get it save Pinkel," said they; for they did not imagine that the witch, after two warnings, could allow their brother to escape a third time. So Pinkel was sent for, and with a glad heart he set out.

He passed many hours inventing first one plan and then another, till he had a scheme ready which he thought might prove successful.

Thrusting a large bag inside his coat he pushed off from the shore, taking care this time to reach the island in daylight. Having made his boat fast to a tree he walked up to the hut, hanging his head and putting on a face that was both sorrowful and ashamed.

"Is that you Pinkel?" asked the witch, when she saw him, her eyes gleaming savagely.

"Yes, dear mother, it is I," answered Pinkel.

"So you have dared, after all you have done, to put yourself in my power!" cried she. "Well, you shan't escape me this time!" and she took down a large knife and began to sharpen it.

"Oh, dear mother, spare me!" shrieked Pinkel, falling on his knees and looking wildly about him.

"Spare you indeed! Where are my lantern and my goat? No! No! There is only one fate for you!" and she brandished the knife in the air so that it glittered in the firelight.

"Then if I must die," said Pinkel who, by this time, was really rather frightened, "let me at least choose the manner of my death. I am very hungry, for I have had nothing to eat all day. Put some poison, if you like, into the porridge, but at least let me have a good meal before I die."

"That is not a bad idea," answered the witch. And ladling out a large bowl of porridge, she stirred some poisonous herbs into it, and set about some work that had to be done. Then Pinkel hastily poured all the contents of the bowl into his bag, and made a great noise with his spoon, as if he was scraping up the last morsel.

"The porridge is excellent. Do give me some more," said Pinkel, turning towards her.

"Well, you have a fine appetite, young man," answered the witch. "However, it is the last time you will eat, so I will give you another bowlful." And stirring in some herbs, she poured him out half of what remained, and went to the window to call her cat.

In an instant Pinkel again emptied the porridge into the bag, and the next minute he rolled on the floor, twisting himself, and uttering loud groans the while. Suddenly he grew silent and lay still.

"Ah! I thought a second dose would be too much for you," said the witch, looking at him. "I warned you what would happen if you came back. But why does not my lazy girl bring the wood I sent her for, it will soon be too dark for her to find her way? I suppose I must go and search for her. What a trouble girls are!"

The witch went to the door to watch if there were any signs of her daughter. But nothing could be seen of her, and heavy rain was falling.

"It is no night for my cloak," she muttered. "It would be covered with mud by the time I got back." So she took it off her shoulders and hung it carefully up in a cupboard in the room. After that she put on her clogs and started to seek her daughter. Directly the last sound of her clogs had ceased, Pinkel jumped up, took down the cloak, and rowed off as fast as he could.

He had not gone far when a puff of wind unfolded the cloak, and its brightness shed gleams across the water. The witch, who was just entering the forest,

turned round at that moment and saw the golden rays. She forgot all about her daughter, and ran down to the shore, screaming with rage at being outwitted a third time.

"Is that you, Pinkel?" cried she.

"Yes, dear mother, it is I."

"Have you taken my golden cloak?"

"Yes, dear mother, I have."

"Are you a great knave?"

"Yes, truly, dear mother, I am."

And so indeed he was!

But, all the same, he carried the cloak to the King's palace, and in return he received the hand of the King's daughter in marriage. People said that it was the bride who ought to have worn the cloak at her wedding feast, but the King was so pleased with it that he would not part from it, and to the end of his life was never seen without it.

After his death, Pinkel became King and ruled his subjects well. As for his brothers, he did not punish them, but left them in the stables, where they grumbled all day long.

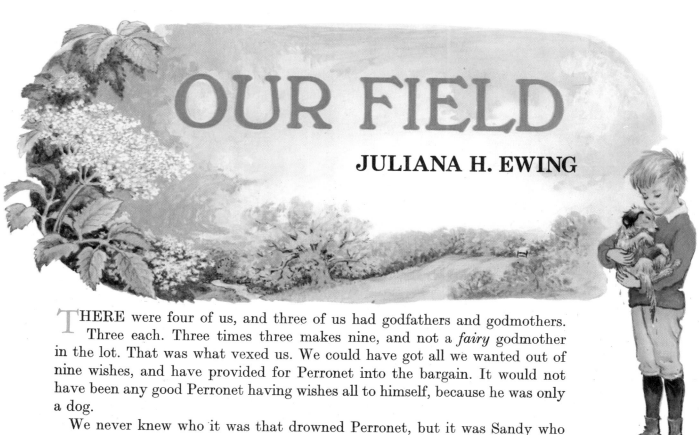

OUR FIELD

JULIANA H. EWING

THERE were four of us, and three of us had godfathers and godmothers. Three each. Three times three makes nine, and not a *fairy* godmother in the lot. That was what vexed us. We could have got all we wanted out of nine wishes, and have provided for Perronet into the bargain. It would not have been any good Perronet having wishes all to himself, because he was only a dog.

We never knew who it was that drowned Perronet, but it was Sandy who saved his life and brought him home. It was when he was coming home from school, and he brought Perronet with him. Perronet was not at all nice to look at when we first saw him, though we were very sorry for him. He was wet all over, and his eyes shut, and you could see his ribs, and he looked quite dark and sticky. But when he dried, he dried a lovely yellow, with two black ears like velvet. People sometimes asked us what kind of dog he was, but we never knew, except that he was the nicest possible kind.

When we had got him, we were afraid we were not going to be allowed to have him. Mother said we could not afford him, because of the tax and his keep. The tax was five shillings, but there wanted nearly a year to the time of paying it. Of course his keep began as soon as he could eat, and that was the very same evening. We were all very miserable, because we were so fond of Perronet—at least, Perronet was not his name then, but he was the same person—and at last it was settled that all three of us would give up sugar, towards saving the expense of his keep, if he might stay. It was hardest for Sandy, because he was particularly fond of sweet things; but then he was particularly fond of Perronet. So we all gave up sugar, and Perronet was allowed to remain.

About the tax, we thought we could save any pennies or halfpennies we got during the year, and it was such a long time to the time for paying, that we should be almost sure to have enough by then. We had not any money at the time, or we should have bought a savings-box; but lots of people save their money in stockings, and we settled that we would. An old stocking would not do, because of the holes, and I had not many good pairs; but we thought we could pour the money into one of my good summer ones when the winter came.

What we most of all wanted a fairy godmother for was about our "homes." There was no kind of play we liked better than playing at houses and new homes. But no matter where we made our "home," it was sure to be disturbed. If it was indoors, and we made a palace under the big table, as soon as ever we had got it nicely divided into rooms according to where the legs came, it was certain to be dinner-time, and people put their feet into it. The nicest house we ever had was in the outhouse; we had it, and kept it quite a secret, for weeks. And then the new load of wood came and covered up everything, our best oyster-shell dinner service and all.

It was one day early in May—a very hot day for the time of year, which had made us rather cross—when Sandy came in about four o'clock, smiling more broadly even than usual, and said to Richard and me, "I've got a fairy god-mother, and she's given us a field."

Sandy was very fond of eating. He used to keep back things from meals to enjoy afterwards. He brought a piece of cake out of his pocket now, and took a large mouthful.

"What's the good of a field?" said Richard.

"It's quite a new place," said Sandy. "You've never been there," and he took a triumphant bite of the cake.

"How did you get there?" asked Richard.

"The fairy godmother showed me," was Sandy's reply. "Come along."

He took us along Gipsy Lane. We had been there once or twice for walks, but not very often. At the end of it there is a stile, by which you go into a field, and at the other end you get over another stile, and find yourself in the high road.

"If this is our field, Sandy," said I, when we got to the first stile, "I'm very sorry, but it really won't do. I know that lots of people come through it. We should never be quiet here."

Sandy didn't speak, and he didn't get over the stile; he went through a gate close by it leading into a little sort of bye-lane that was all mud in winter and hard cart-ruts in summer. I had never been up it, but I had seen hay and that sort of thing go in and come out of it.

He went on and we followed him. The ruts were very disagreeable to walk on, but presently he led us through a hole in the hedge, and we got into a field. There was no path, but Sandy walked away up it, and we went after him. There was another hedge at the top, and a stile in it, and we all climbed over. When we got to the other side, Sandy leaned against the post and gave a wave with his right hand and said, "This is our field."

It sloped downhill, and the hedges round it were rather high, with awkward branches of black-thorn sticking out here and there without any leaves, and with the blossom lying white on the black twigs like snow. There were cowslips all over the field, but they were thicker at the lower end, which was damp. The great heat of the day was over. The sun shone still, but it shone low down and made such splendid shadows that we all walked about with grey giants at our feet; and it made the bright green of the grass, and the cowslips down below, and the top of the hedge, and Sandy's hair, and everything in the sun, and the mist behind the elder-bush which was out of the sun, so yellow—so very yellow —that just for a minute I really believed about Sandy's godmother, and thought it was a story come true, and that everything was turning into gold.

But it was only for a minute; of course, I know that fairy tales are not true. But it was a lovely field, and when we had put our hands to our eyes, and had a good look at it, I said to Sandy, "It is the best field I ever heard of."

"Sit down," said Sandy. "There are violets just behind us. Can't you smell them? But whatever you do, don't tell anybody of those, or we shan't keep our field to ourselves for a day. And look here." He had turned over on to his face, and Richard and I did the same, whilst Sandy fumbled among the bleached grass and brown leaves.

"Hyacinths," said Richard, as Sandy displayed the green tops of them.

"As thick as peas," said Sandy. "This bank will be blue in a few weeks; and fiddle-heads everywhere. There will be no end of ferns. May to any extent—it's only in bud yet—and there's a wren's nest in there—" At this point he rolled suddenly on to his back and looked up. "A lark," he explained; "there was one singing its head off this morning. I say, Dick, this will be a good field for a kite, won't it? *But wait a bit.* There's a brook at the bottom there."

After every fresh thing that Sandy showed us in Our Field, he always finished by saying, "*Wait a bit*," and that was because there was always something else better still.

"It's almost *too* good, Sandy dear," said I, as we crossed the field to the opposite hedge.

"The best is to come," said Sandy. "I've a very good mind not to let it out till to-morrow."

Richard and I tried hard to persuade him to show us everything. After a bit, Sandy, jumping up, said, "One can only tell a secret once. It's a hollow oak. Come along!"

He ran and we ran to the other side of Our Field. I had read of hollow oaks, and seen pictures of them, and once I dreamed of one, with a witch inside, but we had never had one to play in. We were nearly wild with delight. It looked all solid from the field, but when we pushed behind, on the hedge side, there was the door, and I crept in, and it smelt of wood and delicious damp. The light came in from the top, where the polypody hung over like a fringe. Sandy was quite right. It was the best thing in Our Field.

We had all kinds of games in Our Field. Shops—for there were quantities of things to sell—and sometimes I was a moss merchant, for there were ten different kinds of moss by the brook, and sometimes I was a jeweller, and sold daisy-chains and pebbles, and coral sets made of holly berries, and oak-apple necklaces; and sometimes I kept provisions, like earth-nuts, and mallow-cheeses, and mushrooms; and sometimes I kept a flower-shop, and sold nosegays and wreaths, and umbrellas made of rushes. And sometimes I kept a whole lot of shops, and Richard and Sandy bought my things, and paid for them with money made of elder-pith, sliced into rounds. The first shop I kept was to sell cowslips, and Richard and Sandy lived by the brook, and were wine merchants, and made cowslip wine in a tin mug.

The elder tree was a beauty. In July the cream-coloured flowers were so sweet, we could hardly sit under it, and in the autumn it was covered with berries; but we were always a little disappointed that they never tasted in the least like elderberry syrup. Richard used to make flutes out of the stalks, and one really did to play tunes on, but it always made Perronet bark.

We played at castles, and houses, and when we were tired of the houses, we pretended to pack up, and went to the seaside for change of air by the brook. Whatever we played at we were never disturbed. Birds and cows, and men and horses ploughing in the distance, do not disturb you at all.

We were very happy that summer: the boys were quite happy, and the only thing that vexed me was thinking of Perronet's tax-money. For months and months went on and we did not save it. Once we got as far as twopence-half-penny, and then one day Richard came to me and said, "I must have some more string for the kite. You might lend me a penny out of Perronet's stocking till I get some money of my own."

So I did; and the next day Sandy came and said, "You lent Dick one of Perronet's coppers, I'm sure Perronet would lend me one," and then they said it was ridiculous to leave a halfpenny there by itself, so we spent it on acid drops.

It worried me so much at last that I began to dream horrible dreams about Perronet having to go away because we hadn't saved his tax-money. The boys never seemed to mind, but then boys don't think about things; so that I was quite surprised when one day I found Sandy alone in Our Field with Perronet in his arms; and I found he was crying about the tax-money. I said I was quite determined to try and think of something. It certainly was remarkable that the very next day should be the day when we heard about the flower-show.

It was in school—the village school, for mother could not afford to send us anywhere else—and the schoolmaster rapped on his desk, and said, "Silence, children!" and that at the Agricultural Show there was to be a flower-show this year, and that an old gentleman was going to give prizes to the school-children for window-plants and for the best arranged wild-flowers. There was to be a first prize of five shillings and a second prize of half a crown for the best collection of wild-flowers with the names put to them.

"The English names," said the schoolmaster; "and there may be—silence, children!—there may be collections of ferns, or grasses, or mosses to compete, too, for the gentleman wishes to encourage a taste for natural history."

And several of the village children said, "What's that?" I squeezed Sandy's arm, who was sitting next to me, and I thought I never should have finished my lessons that day for thinking of Perronet's tax-money.

July is not at all a good month for wild-flowers; May and June are far better. However, the show was to be in the first week in July.

I said to the boys, "Look here, I'll do a collection of flowers. I know the names, and I can print. It's no good two or three people muddling with arranging flowers; but if you will get me what I want, I shall be very much obliged. If either of you will make another collection, you know there are ten kinds of mosses by the brook; and we have names for them of our own, and they are English. Perhaps they'll do. But everything must come out of Our Field."

The boys agreed, and they were very good. Richard made me a box, rather high at the back. We put sand at the bottom and damped it, and then Feather Moss, lovely clumps of it, and into that I stuck the flowers. They all came out of Our Field. I like to see grass with flowers, and we had very pretty grasses, and between every bunch of flowers I put a bunch of grass of different kinds. I got all the flowers and all the grasses ready first, and printed the names on pieces of cardboard to stick in with them, and then I arranged them. Sandy handed me what I called for, for Richard was busy at the brook making a tray of mosses.

Sandy knew the flowers and the names of them quite as well as I did, of course; we knew everything that lived in Our Field, so when I called, "Ox-eye daisies, cock's-foot grass, labels; meadow-sweet, fox-tail grass, labels; dog-roses, shivering grass, labels;" and so on, he gave me the right things, and I had nothing to do but to put the colours that looked best together next to each other, and pull up bits of the moss to show well. And at the very end I put in a label. "All out of Our Field."

I did not like it when it was done; but Richard praised it so much it cheered me up, and I thought his mosses looked lovely.

The flower-show day was very hot. I did not think it could be hotter anywhere in the world than it was in the field where the show was, but it was hotter in the tent.

We should never have got in at all—for you had to pay at the gate—but they let competitors in free, though not at first. When we got in, there were a lot of grown-up people, and it was very hard work getting along among them, and getting to see the stands. We had struggled slowly all round the tent, and seen all the cucumbers, onions, lettuces, long potatoes, round potatoes, and everything else, when we saw an old gentleman, with spectacles and white hair, standing with two or three ladies. And then we saw three nosegays in jugs, with all the green picked off, and the flowers tied as tightly together as they would go, and then we saw some prettier ones, and then we saw my collection, and it had got a big label in it marked "1st Prize," and next to it came Richard's moss-tray, with the Hair-moss and the Pincushion-moss and the Scale-mosses, and a lot of others with names of our own, and it was marked "2nd Prize." And I gripped one of Sandy's arms just as Richard seized the other, and we both cried, "Perronet is paid for."

There was two and sixpence over. We never had such a feast! And we had it in Our Field. I know that Our Field does not exactly belong to us. I wonder to whom it does belong? Richard says he believes it belongs to the gentleman who lives at the big red house among the trees. But he must be wrong, for we see that gentleman at church every Sunday, but we never saw him in Our Field. And I don't believe anybody could have such a field of their very own and never come to see it from one end of summer to the other.

Clock-O'-Clay

JOHN CLARE

In the cowslip pips I lie,
Hidden from the buzzing fly,
While green grass beneath me lies,
Pearled with dew like fishes' eyes,
Here I lie, a clock-o'-clay,
Waiting for the time o' day.

While the forest quakes surprise,
And the wild wind sobs and sighs,
My home rocks as like to fall,
On its pillar green and tall;
When the pattering rain drives by
Clock-o'-clay keeps warm and dry.

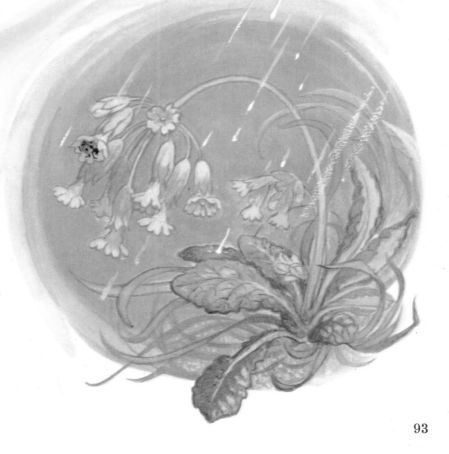

Day by day and night by night,
All the week I hide from sight;
In the cowslip pips I lie,
In the rain still warm and dry;
Day and night, and night and day,
Red, black-spotted clock-o'-clay.

My home shakes in wind and showers,
Pale green pillar topped with flowers,
Bending at the wild wind's breath,
Till I touch the grass beneath;
Here I live, lone clock-o'-clay,
Watching for the time of day.

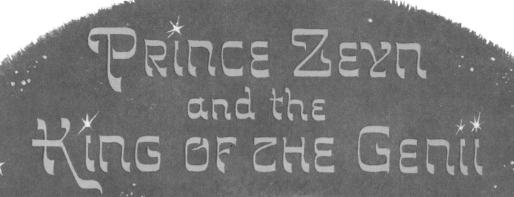

Prince Zeyn and the King of the Genii

A story from The Arabian Nights.

THERE was once a King of Balsora who was very rich and good, and much loved by all the people whom he ruled. He had one son, whose name was Zeyn. Gathering together all the wise men in his country, he asked them to find out what sort of a boy the young Prince would be. So the wise men went out into the palace garden on a fine starlit night, and, looking up at the stars, said they could see wonderful things that would happen to Prince Zeyn.

"The stars say he will be very brave," said one wise man.

"They tell me that he will have strange adventures," said another.

"And he will live to be very old," added a third.

The young Prince grew up, and was taught everything that princes ought to know; but when he was still quite young, his father was taken very ill. Knowing that he was going to die, he sent for Prince Zeyn.

"You will soon be the king of this country," he said. "And I hope you will be a good one. Do not listen to those who are always praising you, and try to find out the real truth before you punish any one."

Prince Zeyn promised to remember his father's words, and afterwards the old king died.

At first Zeyn was not a good king. Being able to do whatever he liked, he spent most of his time in amusing himself and spending money. His mother, a very wise queen, reminded him of his father's words, and he began to feel sorry that he was not a better king, whom his people could love as they had loved his father.

But his money was all spent, and, not knowing where to get any more, he felt sad. One night he had a wonderful dream. He looked up and saw an old man standing beside his bed and smiling kindly down upon him.

"Oh, Zeyn," said the old man, "joy comes after sorrow, and happiness after sadness. The time of your riches has come. Tomorrow morning, take an axe, and dig in your father's room. There you will find a great treasure."

Now Zeyn did not believe this, but, feeling rather curious, he told the Queen his dream, and then, sending for an axe, shut himself up alone in his father's room. He dug up the pavement until he was quite tired, but at last his axe struck against a white stone, which he lifted eagerly.

To his surprise, he found a door fastened with a padlock. The axe soon broke this, and there, before the Prince, a marble staircase went down into the earth. Lighting a taper, Zeyn ran down, to find himself in a fine chamber with a crystal floor. All round it were shelves, and on the shelves ten big urns.

Zeyn took off the lid of the first urn, and found it full of gold. He then looked into the other urns, and behold, every one was full of gold. He took a handful to the Queen, who was greatly astonished, and went with him to the room where the treasure was hidden.

In one corner the Queen saw another little urn, and inside it was nothing but a key. "This must lead to another treasure," they said, and, looking round the room, found a lock in the middle of the wall, which the key just fitted. When it was turned, this door opened, and showed a large hall in which stood eight shining diamond statues upon eight large gold pedestals.

But there was one more pedestal which had no statue, and above it lay a piece of white satin on which Zeyn read these words written by his father: *My dear son, all these statues are for you. Go to Cairo and find an old slave of mine called Mobarec. He will show you a place where you may find a ninth statue more beautiful than all the rest.*

When he had read this, Zeyn set off to discover the ninth statue to fill the empty pedestal. Going to Cairo, he soon found the old slave Mobarec, who was now one of the richest men in the city.

"I am the son of the King of Balsora," said Zeyn.

"And how shall I know that you are speaking the truth?" said the old slave, looking straight into Zeyn's eyes.

"Because I can tell you my father had a secret room in which were ten urns full of gold and eight diamond statues. I have come to you to ask you where to find the ninth."

"You are indeed the young Prince!" cried Mobarec.

The next morning, Zeyn and Mobarec set out on their search for the ninth statue. The old man said that the Prince must be prepared to face many dangers, but as Zeyn was longing for adventures this did not frighten him.

After travelling for many days they came to some tall and waving palm trees, standing all around a lake of shining water. A silver moon looked through the trees and everything was very silent.

"You will now need all your courage," whispered Mobarec. "We are near the dreadful place where the ninth statue is guarded. We shall have to cross this water."

"But we have no boat," answered Zeyn.

"Wait a moment," said Mobarec, "and a fairy boat belonging to the King of the Genii will appear. But, however strange it looks, be very careful not to make a sound. If you speak, we shall all go to the bottom and be drowned."

Mobarec shaded his eyes and looked across the shining water. A little boat came into sight with an amber mast and a floating sail of blue satin. In a moment they had crossed the lake, the only sound being the soft rush of oars in the water.

"We may speak now," said Mobarec. "We are on a beautiful island belonging to the King of the Genii."

Very soon they came in front of an emerald castle with a golden gate, where several tall genii stood as guards. They were the fairies who lived on the island, and were tall and terrible to look at to those who did not understand them. But Mobarec did; so he took from under his robe two little square carpets, one for Zeyn, and one for himself. These were magic carpets, and those who sat on them were quite safe.

"The King of the Genii will be here soon now," said Mobarec. "If he is angry with us for coming, he will look like a monster; but if he is pleased, he will be very handsome."

There was a flash of lightning, a loud noise of thunder, and then all the island went dark. Suddenly a big, fine-looking man stood before them, and began to smile.

"Welcome, Prince Zeyn," he said. "I loved your father, and whenever he came to see me, I gave him a diamond statue for his very own. It was I whom you saw in your dreams, and I promised your father to give you the ninth statue, which is the most beautiful of all.

"But there is only one way to get it. You must search the world until you find a beautiful maiden who is not only clever but who has never in her life spoken an angry word or thought a wicked thought. When you have found her, bring her back here, to wait upon my Queen, and then I will give you the statue."

Zeyn promised to do all this, though he knew it would be a hard task; but he asked the King of the Genii how he should know the maiden.

"Here is a magic mirror," replied the King. "Only the right maiden will be able to see her face in this."

So Mobarec and Prince Zeyn went away into the world again to find a perfect maiden. They gathered together all the beautiful girls in Cairo, but not one of them could see her own face in the mirror. It grew dark and clouded whenever they looked into it. They next went to Baghdad, where they made friends with an old man named Muezin, who told them that he knew the most perfect maiden in the world.

She lived with her father, who had once been a great man at the King's court, but who now spent all his time teaching his daughter to be clever and good. Muezin took Prince Zeyn to see her, and when her father heard that he was the son of the King of Balsora, he was very pleased to see him, and at once allowed his daughter to look into the magic mirror.

The moment she did so, she saw her own lovely face in the shining glass, and every one standing round saw it too. Zeyn had found the perfect maiden that

he sought. Now there was only one way for him to get the maiden, and that was to marry her. Zeyn was quite ready to do this, for she was so good and beautiful that he already loved her. Indeed, he found it very hard to keep his promise, and take her back to the King of the Genii. He thought he would rather have the perfect maiden than the ninth statue.

The King of the magic island was very pleased with the maiden, and said she would be a beautiful slave for his Queen. Then he turned to Prince Zeyn and said, "I am quite satisfied with all you have done. Go home now, and when you reach your palace at Balsora, go down at once into the room where the eight diamond statues are. There you will find the ninth statue, standing on its pedestal."

Prince Zeyn went sadly home with Mobarec, leaving his lovely bride behind him. As soon as he reached the palace he told his mother all that had happened, and she was delighted to hear he would so soon have the ninth statue.

"Come, my son," she said, "let us both go down and look for the new treasure."

Together they went through the stone door, and down the marble staircase. They came to the diamond statues, and there Prince Zeyn stood still in surprise and delight. For the ninth statue was not made of diamonds or gold; it was the beautiful and perfect maiden whom he loved and whom he had been so sad to leave.

The SNOW-CHILD

NATHANIEL HAWTHORNE

ONE afternoon of a cold winter's day, when the sun shone with chilly brightness after a long storm, two children asked leave of their mother to run out and play in the new-fallen snow. The elder child was a little girl called Violet, and her brother was known as Peony, on account of the ruddiness of his round little face. The children lived in a city, and had no wider play-place than a little garden in front of the house, divided by a white fence from the street, and with a pear-tree and two or three plum-trees overshadowing it, and some rose-bushes just in front of the parlour windows. The trees and shrubs, however, were now leafless, and their twigs were enveloped in the light snow.

"Yes, Violet. Yes, Peony," said their mother; "you may go out and play in the new snow."

Out went the two children, with a hop-skip-and-jump that carried them at once into the heart of a huge snowdrift. At last, when they had frosted one another all over with handfuls of snow, Violet was struck with a new idea.

"Peony," said she. "Let's make a figure out of snow—a little snow-girl—and it shall be our sister, and shall run about and play with us all winter. Won't it be nice?"

"Oh, yes!" cried Peony, as plainly as he could speak, for he was a very little boy. "That will be nice!"

"Yes," answered Violet; "Mamma shall see the new little girl. But she must not make her come into the warm parlour; for, you know, our little snow-sister will not like the warmth."

And at once the children began this great business of making a snow-child that should run about. Violet told Peony what to do, while she shaped out all the nicer parts of the snow-figure. It seemed, in fact, not so much to be made by the children, as to grow up under their hands.

"Oh, Violet, how beau-ti-ful she looks!" exclaimed Peony.

"Yes," said Violet. "I did not know, Peony, that we could make such a sweet little girl as this. Now bring me those light wreaths of snow from the lower branches of the pear-tree. I must have them to make our snow-sister's hair."

"Here they are!" answered the little boy. "Take care you do not break them."

"Now," said Violet in a very satisfied voice, "we must have some little shining bits of ice to make the brightness of her eyes."

"Let us call Mamma to look out," said Peony; and then he shouted loudly: "Mamma! Mamma! Mamma! ! ! Look out and see what a nice little girl we are making!"

The mother put down her work for an instant, and looked out of the window. Through the bright, blinding dazzle of the sun and the snow, she saw the two children at work. Indistinctly, she saw the snow-child, and thought to herself that never before was there a snow-figure so cleverly made. She sat down again to her work, and the children, too, kept busily at work in the garden.

"What a nice playmate she will be for us all winter long!" said Violet. "I hope Papa will not be afraid of her giving us a cold! Shan't you love her very much, Peony?"

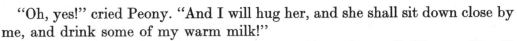

"Oh, yes!" cried Peony. "And I will hug her, and she shall sit down close by me, and drink some of my warm milk!"

"Oh, no, Peony!" answered Violet "That will not do at all. Warm milk will not be good for our little snow-sister. Little snow-people like her eat nothing but icicles."

There was a minute or two of silence; then, all of a sudden, Violet cried out:

"Look, Peony! A light has been shining on her cheek out of that rose-coloured cloud! And the colour does not go away! Isn't that beautiful?"

"Yes; it is beau-ti-ful," answered Peony. "Oh, Violet, look at her hair! It is all like gold!"

"Oh, yes," said Violet. "That colour, you know, comes from the golden clouds that we see up there in the sky."

Just then there came a breeze of the purest west wind, sweeping through the garden and rattling the parlour windows. It sounded so wintry cold, that the mother was about to tap on the window-pane with her thimbled finger to bring the two children in, when they both cried out to her.

"Mamma! Mamma! We have finished our little snow-sister, and she is running about the garden with us! Please look out and see."

The sun had now gone out of the sky and there was not the slightest gleam or dazzle, so that the mother could look all over the garden and see everything and everybody in it. Besides Violet and Peony, there was a small figure of a girl, dressed all in white, with rose-tinged cheeks and ringlets of golden hue, playing about the garden with the two children! The mother thought to herself that it must certainly be the daughter of one of the neighbours, and that, seeing Violet and Peony in the garden, the child had run across the street to play with them. So she went to the door, intending to invite the little runaway into her comfortable parlour. But, after opening the house door, she stood an instant on the threshold, hesitating. Indeed, she almost doubted whether it were a real child, after all, or only a light wreath of the new-fallen snow, blown hither and thither about the garden by the intensely cold west wind. Among all the children of the neighbourhood, the lady could remember no such face, with its pure white and delicate rose-colour. And as for her dress, which was entirely of white and fluttering in the breeze, it was such as no reasonable woman would put on a little girl when sending her out to play in the depth of winter. It made this kind and careful mother shiver only to look at those small feet, with nothing in the world on them except a very thin pair of white slippers. Nevertheless, the child seemed not to feel the cold but danced so lightly over the snow that the tips of her toes left hardly a print on its surface.

Once, in the course of their play, the strange child put herself between Violet and Peony, and took a hand of each; but Peony pulled away his little fist and began to rub it as if the fingers were tingling with cold; while Violet remarked that it was better not to take hold of hands. All this time the mother stood on the threshold, wondering how a little girl could look so much like a flying snowdrift, or how a snowdrift could look so very like a little girl.

She called Violet to her and whispered:

"Violet, my dear, what is this child's name? Does she live near us?"

"Why, Mamma," answered Violet, laughing, "this is our little snow-sister whom we have just been making!"

At this instant a flock of snow-birds came flitting through the air. They flew at once to the snow-child, fluttered eagerly about her head and alighted on her shoulders. She was as glad to see these little birds as they were to see her, and welcomed them by holding out both her hands.

"Violet," said her mother, greatly perplexed, "tell me the truth. Who is this little girl?"

"Mamma," answered Violet, looking into her mother's face, and surprised that she should need any further explanation, "I have told you truly who she is. It is our little snow-figure which Peony and I have been making."

While Mamma still hesitated what to think and what to do, the street-gate was thrown open and the father of Violet and Peony appeared, a fur cap drawn down over his ears and the thickest of gloves on his hands. His eyes brightened at the sight of his wife and children, although he could not help uttering a word or two of surprise at finding the whole family in the open air on so bleak a day, and after sunset too. He soon perceived the little white stranger, and the flock of snow-birds fluttering above her head.

"What little girl is this?" he inquired. "Surely her mother must be crazy to let her go out in such bitter weather with only that flimsy white dress and those thin slippers!"

"My dear," said his wife, "I know no more about the little thing than you do. Some neighbour's child, I suppose. Our Violet and Peony," she added, "insist that she is nothing but a snow-figure which they have been busy making in the garden almost all the afternoon."

As she said that, the mother glanced towards the spot where the children's snow-figure had been made. What was her surprise to see not the slightest trace of so much labour! No piled-up heap of snow! Only the prints of little footsteps around an empty space!

"This is very strange!" said she.

"What is strange?" asked Violet. "Father, do you not see how it is? This is our snow-figure which Peony and I have made because we wanted another playmate."

"Pooh, nonsense, child!" cried their father. "Do not tell me of making live figures out of snow. Come, wife; this little stranger must not stay out in the cold a moment longer. We will bring her into the parlour; and you shall give her a supper of warm bread and milk, and make her as comfortable as you can. Meanwhile I will inquire among the neighbours; or, if necessary, send the city-crier about the streets to give notice of a lost child."

"Father," cried Violet, putting herself before him, "it is true what I have been telling you! This is our little snow-girl, and she cannot live unless she breathes the cold west wind. Do not make her come into the hot room!"

"Nonsense, child, nonsense, nonsense!" cried the father. "Run into the house this moment! It is too late to play any longer. I must take care of this little girl immediately, or she will catch her death of cold!"

The little white creature fled backwards, shaking her head as if to say, "Please do not touch me!"

Some of the neighbours, seeing him from their windows, wondered what could possess the poor man to be running about his garden in pursuit of a snowdrift. At length, he chased the little stranger into a corner where she could not possibly escape him. His wife had been looking on, and, it being nearly twilight, was wonder-struck to observe how the snow-child gleamed and sparkled, and when driven into the corner, she positively glistened like a star!

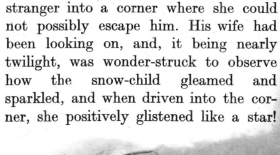

"Come, you odd little thing!" cried the children's father, seizing her by the hand, and with a smile, he led the snow-child towards the house. As she followed him, all the glow and sparkle went out of her figure and she looked as dull and drooping as a thaw.

Violet and Peony, their eyes full of tears, entreated him not to bring their snow-sister into the house.

"Not bring her in!" exclaimed the kind-hearted man. "Why she is so cold, already, that her hand has almost frozen mine, in spite of my thick gloves. Would you have her freeze to death?"

The little white figure was led—drooping more and more—out of the frosty air, and into the comfortable parlour. A stove, filled to the brim with intensely burning coal, was sending a bright gleam through the glass of its iron door. The parlour was hung with red curtains and covered with a red carpet, and looked just as warm as it felt.

The father placed the snow-child on the hearth-rug, right in front of the hissing and fuming stove.

"Now she will be comfortable!" he cried, rubbing his hands and looking about him with the pleasantest smile you ever saw.

Sad, sad and drooping, looked the little white maiden as she stood on the hearth-rug with the hot blast of the stove striking through her. Once she threw a glance towards the windows and caught a glimpse of the snow-covered roofs, and the stars glimmering frostily.

"Come, wife, give her some warm supper as soon as the milk boils," said the good man and turning the collar of his coat up over his ears, he went out of the house, and had barely reached the street-gate when he was recalled by the screams of Violet and Peony.

"Husband! Husband!" cried his wife. "There is no need of going for the child's parents."

"We told you so, Father!" screamed Violet and Peony, as he re-entered the parlour. "You *would* bring her in; and now our poor—dear—little snow-sister is thawed!"

In the utmost perplexity, he demanded an explanation of his wife. She could only reply, that, being brought to the parlour by the cries of Violet and Peony, she found no trace of the little white maiden, except a heap of snow, which, while she was gazing at it, melted quite away upon the hearth-rug.

"And there you see all that is left of it!" added she, pointing to a pool of water in front of the stove.

"Yes, Father," said Violet, looking reproachfully at him through her tears, "there is all that is left of our dear little snow-sister!"

"Naughty Father!" cried Peony.

But there is no teaching anything to sensible men like Violet and Peony's father. They know everything that has been, and everything that is, and everything that possibly can be, and they will not recognise a miracle even if it come to pass under their very noses.

"Wife," said the children's father, after being silent for a time, "see what a quantity of snow the children have brought in on their feet! It has made quite a puddle here before the stove. Tell Dora to bring some towels and mop it up!"

THE SELFISH GIANT

OSCAR WILDE

EVERY afternoon, as they were coming from school, the children used to go and play in the Giant's garden. It was a large, lovely garden, with soft green grass. Here and there over the grass stood beautiful flowers like stars, and there were twelve peach-trees that in the springtime broke out into delicate blossoms of pink and pearl, and in the autumn bore rich fruit. The birds sat on the trees and sang so sweetly that the children used to stop their games in order to listen to them.

"How happy we are here!" they cried to each other.

One day the Giant came back. He had been to visit his friend the Cornish Ogre and had stayed with him for seven years. After the seven years were over he had said all that he had to say, for his conversation was limited, and he determined to return to his own castle. When he arrived he saw the children playing in the garden.

"What are you doing here?" he cried in a very gruff voice, and the children ran away.

"My own garden is my own garden," said the Giant; "anyone can understand that, and I will allow nobody to play in it but myself."

So he built a high wall all round it, and put up a notice board.

He was a very selfish Giant.

108

The poor children had now nowhere to play. They tried to play on the road, but the road was very dusty and full of hard stones, and they did not like it. They used to wander round the high walls when their lessons were over, and talk about the beautiful garden inside.

"How happy we were there!" they said to each other.

Then the Spring came, and all over the country there were little blossoms and little birds. Only in the garden of the Selfish Giant it was still winter. The birds did not care to sing in it as there were no children, and the trees forgot to blossom. Once a beautiful flower put its head out from the grass, but when it saw the notice board it was so sorry for the children that it slipped back into the ground again, and went off to sleep. The only people who were pleased were the Snow and the Frost.

"Spring has forgotten this garden," they cried, "so we will live here all the year round."

The Snow covered up the grass with her great white cloak, and the Frost painted all the trees silver. Then they invited the North Wind to stay with them and he came. He was wrapped in furs, and he roared all day about the garden, and blew the chimney-pots down.

"This is a delightful spot," he said, "we must ask the Hail on a visit."

So the Hail came. Every day for three hours he rattled on the roof of the castle till he broke most of the slates, and then he ran round and round the garden as fast as he could go. He was dressed in grey and his breath was like ice.

"I cannot understand why the Spring is so late in coming," said the Selfish Giant, as he sat at the window and looked out at his cold, white garden; "I hope there will be a change in the weather."

But the Spring never came, nor the Summer. The Autumn gave golden fruit

to every garden, but to the Giant's garden she gave none. "He is too selfish," she said. So it was always winter there, and the North Wind and the Hail, and the Frost and the Snow, danced about through the trees.

One morning the Giant was lying awake in bed when he heard some lovely music. It sounded so sweet to his ears that he thought it must be the King's musicians passing by. It was really only a little linnet singing outside the window, but it was so long since he had heard a bird sing in his garden that it seemed to him to be the most beautiful music in the world. Then the Hail stopped dancing over his head, and the North Wind ceased roaring, and a delicious perfume came to him through the open casement.

"I believe the Spring has come at last," said the Giant; and he jumped out of bed and looked out.

What did he see?

He saw a most wonderful sight. Through a little hole in the wall the children had crept in, and they were sitting in the branches of the trees. In every tree that he could see there was a little child. And the trees were so glad to have the children back again that they had covered themselves with blossoms, and were waving their arms gently above the children's heads. The birds were flying about and twittering with delight, and the flowers were looking up through the green grass and laughing. It was a lovely scene, only in one corner it was still winter. It was the farthest corner of the garden, and in it was standing a little boy. He was so small that he could not reach up to the branches of the tree, and he was wandering all round it, crying bitterly. The poor tree was still covered with frost and snow, and the North Wind was blowing and roaring above it.

"Climb up! little boy," said the Tree, and it bent its branches down as low as it could; but the boy was too tiny.

And the Giant's heart melted as he looked out. "How selfish I have been!" he said; "Now I know why the Spring would not come here. I will put that poor little boy on the top of the tree, and then I will knock down the wall, and my garden shall be the children's playground for ever and ever."

He was really very sorry for what he had done.

So he crept downstairs and opened the front door quite softly, and went out into the garden. But when the children saw him they were so frightened that they all ran away, and the garden became winter again. Only the little boy did not run for his eyes were so full of tears that he did not see the Giant coming. And the Giant stole up behind him and took him gently in his hand, and put him up into the tree. And the tree broke at once into blossom, and the birds came and sang on it, and the little boy stretched out his two arms and

111

flung them round the Giant's neck, and kissed him. And the other children, when they saw that the Giant was not wicked any longer, came running back, and with them came the Spring.

"It is your garden now, little children," said the Giant, and he took a great axe and knocked down the wall.

And when the people were going to market at twelve o'clock they found the Giant playing with the children in the most beautiful garden they had ever seen. All day long they played, and in the evening they came to the Giant to bid him good-bye.

"But where is your little companion?" he said; "the boy I put into the tree." The Giant loved him the best because he had kissed him.

"We don't know," answered the children; "he has gone away."

"You must tell him to come to-morrow," said the Giant. But the children said that they did not know where he lived, and had never seen him before; and the Giant felt very sad.

Every afternoon, when school was over, the children came and played with the Giant. But the little boy whom the Giant loved was never seen again. The Giant was very kind to all the children, yet he longed for his first little friend. "How I would like to see him!" he used to say.

Years went over, and the Giant grew very old and feeble. He could not play about any more, so he sat in a huge armchair and watched the children at their games, and admired his garden. "I have many beautiful flowers," he said, "but the children are the most beautiful flowers of all."

One winter morning he looked out of his window as he was dressing. He did not hate the Winter now, for he knew that it was merely the Spring asleep, and that the flowers were resting.

Suddenly he rubbed his eyes in wonder and looked and looked. In the farthest corner of the garden was a tree quite covered with lovely white blossoms, its branches were golden, and silver fruit hung down from them, and underneath it stood the little boy he had loved.

Downstairs ran the Giant in great joy, and out into the garden. He hastened across the grass, and came near to the child. And when he came quite close his face grew red with anger, and he said, "Who hath dared to wound thee?" For on the palms of the child's hands were the prints of two nails, and the prints of two nails were on the little feet. "Who hath dared to wound thee?" cried the Giant; "tell me, that I may take my big sword and slay him."

"Nay," answered the child; "but these are the wounds of Love."

"Who art thou?" said the Giant, and a strange awe fell on him, and he knelt before the little child.

And the child smiled on the Giant, and said to him, "You let me play once in your garden, to-day you shall come with me to my garden, which is Paradise."

And when the children ran in that afternoon, they found the Giant lying dead under the tree, all covered with white blossoms.

TOM

CHARLES KINGSLEY

ONCE upon a time there was a little chimney-sweep, and his name was Tom.

Now I dare say you never got up at three o'clock on a midsummer morning. Some people get up then because they want to catch salmon; and some, because they want to climb the Alps; and a great many more, because they must, like Tom.

One day a smart little groom rode into the court where Tom lived and halloed to him to know where Mr. Grimes, the chimney-sweep, lived. Mr. Grimes was to come up next morning to Sir John Harthover's at the Place, for his old chimney-sweep was gone to prison, and the chimneys wanted sweeping.

So Tom and his master set out; Grimes rode the donkey in front, and Tom and the brushes walked behind; out of the court, and up the street, past the closed window shutters, and the winking weary policemen, and the roofs all shining grey in the grey dawn. On they went; and Tom looked, and looked, for he never had been so far into the country before.

Soon they came up with a poor Irishwoman, trudging along with a bundle at her back. She had neither shoes nor stockings, and limped along as if she were tired and footsore. Mr. Grimes called out to her.

"This is a hard road. Will ye up and ride behind me?"

But she answered quietly: "No thank you; I'd sooner walk with your little lad here."

So she walked beside Tom and talked to him and asked him where he lived, and what he knew, and all about himself, till Tom thought he had never met such a pleasant-spoken woman. Then he asked her where she lived; and she said far away by the sea. And Tom asked her about the sea; and she told him how it rolled and roared over the rocks in winter nights, and lay still in the bright summer days, for the children to bathe and play in it; and many a story more, till Tom longed to go and see the sea, and bathe in it likewise.

At last, at the bottom of a hill, they came to a spring and there Grimes stopped. Without a word, he got off his donkey, and clambered over the low wall, and knelt down, and began dipping his ugly head into the spring.

"I wish I might go and dip my head in," said poor little Tom.

"Thou come along," said Grimes, "what dost want with washing thyself?" Grimes was very sulky, because the woman preferred Tom's company to his; so he dashed at Tom and began beating him.

"Are you not ashamed of yourself, Thomas Grimes?" cried the Irishwoman over the wall.

Grimes looked up, startled at her knowing his name; but all he answered was, "No: nor never was yet;" and went on beating Tom.

"Stop!" said the Irishwoman. "If you strike that boy again, I can tell what I know. I have one more word for you both.

Those that wish to be clean,
Clean they will be;
And those that wish to be foul,
Foul they will be.

Remember."

And she turned away and through a gate into the meadow. Grimes rushed after her, shouting, "You come back!" But when he got into the meadow the woman was not there. There was no place to hide in, but look where he would, she was not there.

They had gone three miles and more, and came to Sir John's lodge-gates. Grimes rang at the gate, and out came a keeper on the spot and opened. They walked up a great lime avenue, a full mile long, and between their stems Tom peeped trembling at the horns of the sleeping deer, which stood up among the ferns. Tom had never seen such enormous trees, and as he looked up he fancied that the blue sky rested on their heads.

"I wish I were a keeper," said Tom, "to live in such a beautiful place, and wear green velveteens and have a real dog-whistle at my button, like you."

The keeper laughed; he was a kind-hearted fellow.

By this time they were come up to the great iron gates in front of the house; and Tom stared through them at the house itself, and wondered how many chimneys there were in it.

But Tom and his master did not go in through the great iron gates, as if they had been Dukes or Bishops, but round the back way, and a very long way round it was; and into a little back door, where the ash-boy let them in, yawning horribly; and then in a passage the housekeeper met them, and she gave Grimes solemn orders about, "You will take care of this, and take care of that."

And Grimes listened, and said every now and then, under his voice, "You'll mind that, you little beggar?" and Tom did mind, all at least that he could. And then the housekeeper turned them into a grand room, all covered up in sheets of brown paper, and bade them begin in a lofty and tremendous voice; and so, after a whimper or two, and a kick from his master, into the grate Tom went, and up the chimney.

How many chimneys he swept I cannot say; but he swept so many that he got quite tired, and puzzled too, for they were not like the town flues to which he was accustomed, but such as you would find—if you would only get up them and look, which perhaps you would not like to do—in old country houses; large and crooked chimneys, which had been altered again and again, till they ran into one another. So Tom fairly lost his way in them; not that he cared much for that, though he was in pitchy darkness, for he was as much at home in a chimney as a mole is underground; but at last, coming down, as he thought, the right chimney, he came down the wrong one, and found himself standing on the hearthrug in a room the like of which he had never seen before.

The room was all dressed in white; white window curtains, white bed curtains, white furniture, and white walls, with just a few lines of pink here and there. The carpet was all over gay little flowers; and the walls were hung with pictures in gilt frames. There were pictures of ladies and gentlemen and pictures of horses and dogs.

The next thing he saw, and that puzzled him, was a washing-stand, with ewers and basins, and soap and brushes, and towels; and a large bath, full of clean water—what a heap of things all for washing! "She must be a very dirty lady," thought Tom, "to want as much scrubbing as all that."

And then, looking towards the bed, he saw that dirty lady, and held his breath with astonishment. Under the snow-white coverlet, upon the snow-white pillow, lay the most beautiful little girl that Tom had ever seen. Her cheeks were almost as white as the pillow, and her hair was like threads of gold spread all about over the bed. She might have been as old as Tom, or maybe a year or two older; but Tom did not think of that. He thought only of her delicate skin and golden hair, and wondered whether she were a real live person, or one of the wax dolls he had seen in the shops. But when he saw her breathe, he made up his mind that she was alive, and stood staring at her, as if she had been an angel out of heaven.

And then he thought, "And are all people like that when they are washed?"
And he looked at his own wrist, and tried to rub the soot off, and wondered
whether it ever would come off. And looking round he suddenly saw, standing
close to him, a little ugly, black, ragged figure, with bleared eyes and grinning
white teeth. He turned on it angrily. What did such a little black ape want in
that sweet young lady's room? And behold, it was himself, reflected in a
great mirror, the like of which Tom had never seen before.

And Tom, for the first time in his life, found out that he was dirty; and
burst into tears with shame and anger; and turned to sneak up the chimney
again and hide, and upset the fender, and threw the fire-irons down, with a
noise as of ten thousand tin kettles tied to ten thousand mad dogs' tails.

Up jumped the little white lady in her bed, and, seeing Tom, screamed as
shrill as any peacock. In rushed a stout old nurse from the next room, and seeing
Tom, likewise made up her mind that he had come to rob, plunder, destroy,
and burn; and dashed at him as he lay over the fender, so fast that she caught
him by the jacket. But she did not hold him. Tom had been in a policeman's
hands many a time, and out of them too, what is more; so he doubled under
the good lady's arm, across the room, and out of the window in a moment.

But all under the window spread a tree, and down the tree he went, like a cat, and across the garden lawn, and over the iron railings, and up the park towards the wood, leaving the old nurse to scream murder and fire at the window.

The under gardener, mowing, saw Tom and threw down his scythe; and gave chase to poor Tom. The dairy-maid heard the noise, and gave chase to Tom. A groom, cleaning Sir John's hack at the stables, gave chase to Tom. Grimes ran out and gave chase to Tom. The old steward opened the park gate and gave chase to Tom. The ploughman left his horses and gave chase to Tom. The keeper ran after Tom. Sir John looked out of his study window, and up at the nurse, and he ran out and gave chase to Tom. The Irishwoman, too, was walking up to the house to beg; but she threw away her bundle and gave chase to Tom likewise. All ran up the park, shouting, "Stop thief!"

Tom, of course, made for the wood. He was sharp enough to know that he might hide in a bush, or swarm up a tree, and altogether, had more chance there than in the open. But when he got into the wood, the boughs laid hold of his legs and arms, the hassock-grass and sedges tumbled him over and the birches birched him.

"I must get out of this," thought Tom. And indeed I don't think he would ever have got out at all if he had not suddenly run his head against a wall. He guessed that over the wall the cover would end; and up it he went, and over like a squirrel. And there he was, out on the great grouse-moors, heather and bog and rock, stretching away and up, up to the very sky.

At last he came to a dip in the land, and went to the bottom of it, and then he turned bravely away from the wall and up the moor; for he knew that he had put a hill between him and his enemies, and could go on without their seeing him. But the Irishwoman, alone of them all, had seen which way Tom went.

So Tom went on, and on, he hardly knew why. What would Tom have said, if he had seen, walking over the moor behind him, the very same Irishwoman who had taken his part upon the road?

And now he began to get a little hungry, and very thirsty; but he could see nothing to eat anywhere, and still less to drink.

To his right rose moor after moor, hill after hill, till they faded away, blue into blue sky. But between him and those moors, and really at his very feet, lay something, to which, as soon as Tom saw it, he determined to go, for that was the place for him.

A deep, deep green and rocky valley, very narrow, and filled with wood; but through the wood, hundreds of feet below him, he could see a clear stream glance. Oh, if he could but get down to that stream! Then, by the stream, he saw the roof of a little cottage, and a little garden, set out in squares and beds. And there was a tiny little red thing moving in the garden, no bigger than a fly. As Tom looked down, he saw that it was a woman in a red petticoat! Ah! perhaps she would give him something to eat; and he could get down there in five minutes.

But Tom was wrong about getting down in five minutes, for the cottage was more than a mile off, and a good thousand feet below. However, down he went, though he was very footsore, and tired, and hungry, and thirsty, and all the while he never saw the Irishwoman going down behind him. At last he got to the bottom, and stumbled away, down over a low wall, and into a narrow road, and up to the cottage door. And a neat pretty cottage it was, with clipped yew hedges all round the garden, and yews inside too, cut into peacocks and trumpets and teapots and all kinds of queer shapes. He came slowly up to the open door, which was all hung round with clematis and roses; and then peeped in, half afraid.

And there sat by the empty fire-place, which was filled with a pot of sweet herbs, the nicest old woman that ever was seen, in her red petticoat, and short dimity bedgown, and clean white cap, with a black silk handkerchief over it, tied under her chin.

Such a pleasant cottage it was, with a shiny clean stone floor, and curious old prints on the wall, and an old black oak sideboard full of bright pewter and brass dishes, and a cuckoo clock in the corner, which began shouting as soon as Tom appeared: not that it was frightened at Tom, but that it was just eleven o'clock.

"What are thou, and what dost want?" cried the old dame. "A chimney-sweep! Away with thee. I'll have no sweeps here."

"Water," said poor little Tom, quite faint.

The old dame looked at him through her spectacles one minute and two, and three; and then she said: "He's sick; and a bairn's a bairn, sweep or none."

"Water," said Tom.

"God forgive me!" and she put by her spectacles, and rose, and came to Tom. "Water's bad for thee; I'll give thee milk."

Tom drank the milk off at one draught.

"Bless thy pretty heart! Come wi' me, and I'll hap thee up somewhere."

She put him in an outhouse upon soft sweet hay and an old rug, and bade him sleep. But Tom did not fall asleep. Instead of it he turned and tossed and kicked about in the strangest way, and felt so hot all over that he longed to get into the river and cool himself; and then he fell half asleep, and dreamt that he heard the little white lady crying to him, "Oh, you're so dirty; go and be washed;" and then that he heard the Irishwoman saying, "Those that wish to be clean, clean they will be." And he said out loud again, though being half asleep he did not know it, "I must be clean, I must be clean."

And all of a sudden he found himself, not in the outhouse on the hay, but in the middle of a meadow, over the road, with a stream just before him, saying continually, "I must be clean, I must be clean." He had got there on his own legs, between sleep and awake, as children will often get out of bed, and go about the room, when they are not quite well. But he was not a bit surprised, and went on to the bank of the brook, and lay down on the grass, and looked into the clear, clear limestone water, with every pebble at the bottom bright and clean, while the little silver trout dashed about in fright at the sight of his black face; and he dipped his hand in and found it so cool, cool, cool; and he said, "I will be a fish; I will swim in the water; I must be clean, I must be clean."

So he pulled off all his clothes in such haste that he tore some of them, which was easy enough with such ragged old things. And he put his poor, hot, sore feet into the water; and then his legs. He was so hot and thirsty, and longed so to be clean for once, that he tumbled himself as quick as he could into the clear cool stream.

And he had not been in it two minutes before he fell fast asleep, into the quietest, sunniest, cosiest sleep that ever he had in his life; and he dreamt about the green meadows by which he had walked that morning, and the tall elm trees, and the sleeping cows; and after that he dreamt of nothing at all. The reason of his falling into such a delightful sleep is very simple. It was merely that the fairies took him.

And now comes the most wonderful part of this wonderful story. Tom, when he woke, for, of course, he woke, found himself swimming about in the stream, being about four inches long, and having a set of gills which he mistook for a lace frill, till he pulled at them, found he hurt himself, and made up his mind that they were part of himself and best left alone. In fact the fairies had turned him into a water baby.

A water baby? You never heard of a water baby? Perhaps not. That is the very reason why this story was written. There are a great many things in the world which you never heard of; and a great many more which nobody ever heard of; and a great many things too, which nobody will ever hear of.

But at all events, so it happened to Tom. And, therefore, the keeper, and the groom, and Sir John, made a great mistake, and were very unhappy (Sir John at least) without any reason, when they found a black thing in the water, and said it was Tom and that he had been drowned. They were utterly mistaken. Tom was quite alive; and cleaner, and merrier, than he ever had been. The fairies had washed him, you see, in the swift river, so thoroughly that not only his dirt, but his whole husk and shell had been washed quite off him, and the pretty little real Tom was washed out of the inside of it, and swam away.

But good Sir John did not understand all this, and he took it into his head that Tom was drowned. And all the while Tom was swimming about in the river, with a pretty little lace-collar of gills about his neck, as lively as a grig, and as clean as a fresh-run salmon.